PARKLAND COLLE

9780805475050

DRAMA FOR FUN

Cecil McGee

BROADMAN PRESS
Nashville, Tennessee

215472

© Copyright 1969 • BROADMAN PRESS

All rights reserved

Third Printing

ISBN-0-8054-4275-05

Dewey Decimal classification number: 791.1

Library of Congress catalog card number: 69-14368
Printed in the United States of America
4.S7016

To
*my mother, seven brothers, and my sister
who helped make my childhood
one continuous fun drama!*

PREFACE

Few activities can gain as much wholehearted participation as can fun drama. A dozen or more people can easily be involved in preparing even the simplest skit or stunt, and a roomful of people of all ages can be led to active participation by dividing them into small groups and sending them aside to create a brief drama from a given humorous situation. Most of those who once discover the joy of taking part will no longer be content to sit and watch.

Skits, stunts, melodrama, mock opera, and other types of fun drama have a real place in recreation. In light of the growing tendency for people to merely sit and watch, this type of activity is needed to encourage participation and to establish an atmosphere of informality, warmth, and friendliness.

In the process of working on a skit or stunt, barriers are broken down and individuals really get to know one another. Those who feel unwanted find acceptance. The lonely discover the warmth of companionship, and the shy see that they too have something to contribute.

The chief problem encountered in doing fun drama is that of finding suitable material. This book has been put together in an effort to supply the very best fun scripts available and to encourage groups to create their own.

It has long been a dream of mine that someday I might have in one volume the fun drama pieces I like best. DRAMA FOR FUN fulfils that dream! The material included has been chosen with the belief that comedy should be clean and in good taste, regardless of where it is presented. The pieces being shared have been used with both large and small audiences and have been enthusiastically received.

Acknowledgments

I am grateful to the many people who have contributed to this book. It has been my desire to give credit to each person whose material has been used. This is difficult in the area of skits and stunts, since so many pieces have been passed along from one person to another without any knowledge as to who wrote them. I will welcome information in regard to credits that may have been omitted and will include them in a future edition.

Special gratitude is expressed to Bob Boyd and the entire Recreation Department of the Baptist Sunday School Board without whose help this book would not have been possible.

I am indebted to Adelle Carlson who read and edited much of the manuscript and gave invaluable guidance.

Grateful acknowledgment is due the Baptist Sunday School Board for permission to use materials that first appeared in the *Church Recreation* magazine.

A special word of appreciation goes to Agnes Durant Pylant who has inspired and influenced so much of what has gone into this volume.

CECIL McGEE

Contents

1. Fun with Drama **11**
2. Fun with Novelty Stunts **14**
3. Fun with Prepared Skits **38**
4. Fun with Melodrama **78**
5. Fun with Musical Skits **96**
6. Fun with Audience Participation Skits **131**
7. Fun with Choral Speaking **147**
8. Fun with Impromptu Skits **163**

Index **173**

CHAPTER ONE

DRAMA

There is nothing more effective than a skit or stunt to liven up a program. There's a place for fun drama in camps, retreats, school assemblies, club meetings, scouting programs, banquets, parties, picnics, and fellowships.

Skits and stunts are so closely related that it is sometimes difficult to distinguish one from the other. In this book, the term "skit" usually refers to a written script that requires rehearsals, memorization of lines, and other preparation that is required of a play.

The term "stunt" as used in this book more often refers to brief pieces that are done spontaneously and without rehearsals. The only advance preparation necessary is that which must be made by the stunt leader. The term "stunt" can also be used for a trick or a physical accomplishment. Many times, however, the terms "stunt" and "skit" are used interchangeably.

Choosing the Material to be Used

You are well on the road to successful skit production if a good piece of fun drama material has been selected. Consider the following in making a choice:

1. Is the fun drama appropriate for the age group that will present it?
2. Is it appropriate for those who are to see it?
3. Can it be effectively staged in the space and time limitations where it is to be done?
4. Is the material inherently funny and a fresh experience for

the group?

5. Is it worthwhile, suitable for the occasion, and free from anything suggestive and off-color?

6. Is it in good taste in that it does not ridicule or embarrass anyone?

Some of the best material is that which the local group creates, woven around the people and events they know most about.

Preparing the Material to be Used

Here are some basic guidelines to help you in casting and rehearsing the chosen piece:

1. Study the material you have chosen until it comes to life for you! You must be able to see it in mental pictures before you can motivate others to see it. Visualize every tiny detail in working for a smooth production.

2. If the chosen piece is a skit, decide how many rehearsals will be necessary even before you line up the cast. Most groups never allow enough time for adequate preparation. The number of rehearsals will depend upon the ability of the cast and your ability and experience in working with people.

In enlisting the cast, let them know that it is going to be fun plus a lot of hard work. Tell them how many rehearsals will be involved and challenge them to give their best.

3. If it is a new venture for your group, you may need to handpick the cast. Be assured that after a successful performance many people will want in on the fun.

4. Work from the very beginning to make sure that the lines are heard and clearly understood. If the lines are lost, the whole purpose is missed. Projection and careful enunciation will need to be worked on in every rehearsal. This will be especially necessary when doing musical skits. Amateurs seem to have more difficulty in getting the message across through singing than they do in speaking.

5. Make the rehearsals fun! Nobody wants to be in on something dull!

The Presentation

1. Be sure that the audience can see. When a stage is not available, bring in platforms or work "in the round." Rearrange the chairs in the audience for the best sight lines.

2. Point up humor with adequate emphases and pauses. Expect laughter and wait for it.

3. In audience participation stunts, give clear instructions. Share all the necessary information before beginning.

4. When the nature of the stunt makes it possible, demonstrate the piece before asking the audience to do it. Clap Rhythm in chapter 2 is an example of how this can be done.

5. Make the skits and stunts move quickly! If they drag, people lose interest.

6. Give careful consideration to the placement of skits and stunts in relationship to the other elements of the program. The entire program should build in excitement, rather than drop toward the end. A good skit or stunt can be counted on to furnish the peak of fun in the average program.

7. In doing unrehearsed stunts, it is vital that the right people be chosen from the audience. If you do not know the people, count on the audience to choose them. In nearly every case, the audience will choose the most likely people if told the necessary requirements.

8. Stand up before the audience with an air of expectancy. The people you are to lead are ready and willing to have fun and will meet you halfway. Move toward the goal of drama for fun—for all!

CHAPTER TWO

NOVELTY STUNTS

The following "quickie" stunts are favorites of the author which he has personally used and found highly successful. They require no rehearsals, but the leader will need to be entirely familiar with each piece to be used and will want to make certain that needed props are at hand.

The Shaving Stunt

Call to the front of the room four boys and four girls who are favorites of the group. Seat the boys on chairs, facing the audience. Ask each girl to choose a boy and stand behind his chair. Blindfold the girls and then inform them that they are to shave the fellows. Hastily add that they are to use a plastic spoon for the razor. Before giving the signal to start, be sure that the girls understand the following instructions:

1. Place towel around boy's neck
2. Walk back to designated spot where a helper will put shaving cream in your hand
3. Put lather on boy's face
4. Shave it off
5. Go to designated spot and dampen washcloth in pan of water
6. Wash boy's face
7. Go to designated spot for shaving lotion
8. Put shaving lotion on boy
9. Indicate when finished and take off blindfold

Be sure that the girls stand behind the chairs or to the side of the boys so the audience can see.

Washing an Elephant[1]

Call from the audience three people whom you know to be dramatically inclined and good sports. Send them out of the room —far enough away that they cannot hear what's being said. Tell the audience that when you call the first victim in you are going to pantomime washing an elephant. Call the first victim in and tell him to carefully observe every detail, for he will be expected to repeat the process for the second victim when he is called in. Only the leader and the audience know what is being pantomimed. The three victims are given no hints except what they see done in pantomime. When the third person has had his turn, ask him to tell what he thought he was doing. Then ask No. 2 and No. 1 the same question.

The person who leads the stunt must do some practicing ahead so he can visualize an elephant and let the audience know by his clear, distinct pantomime exactly what he is doing. Decide ahead of time where the bucket, mop, and water faucet will be. Practice using them so that the pantomime is clear. Work with the imaginary elephant so the audience will know when you're washing an ear, the trunk, a leg, etc.

An alternate idea that has been effectively used is the bathing of a baby.

The Only One in Captivity

Tell the audience that you're going to bring into the room the most hideous looking creature in captivity. This creature has

[1]Shared by Leon Mitchell, Church Recreation Department, Baptist Sunday School Board, Nashville, Tennessee.

been booked in the major cities on the globe as the eighth wonder of the world! His hideous face makes Frankenstein look like Prince Charming.

Inform the audience that by special arrangements the creature has been flown in and will now make his appearance. Get one of your helpers to lead the creature in. He is covered with a blanket or sheet so that he cannot be seen. He stands with his back to the audience. Tell the people that you're going to let only three or four see the creature. Ask for volunteers. (These have been hand-picked ahead of time and know that they are to walk around behind the creature, lift up the blanket, react in horror, and run out of the room screaming. This must be honestly played or it will weaken the effect.)

When your helpers have had their turn, say that you're going to let one other person see the creature—and that the audience will do the choosing. Be sure a favorite person is chosen. He comes to front and takes a look, just as the others have done, but when the creature sees him, the creature screams and runs away.

Miss America

Ask the girls in the audience to choose four boys who are the very best sports they know. Bring them to the front of the room. Then ask each boy to choose two girls to work with him. When all are assembled at the front, inform the girls that they are to be given ten minutes to fix up their teen-age boy as next year's "Miss America." They are to use only newspapers, scissors, and straight pins. Assign them to rooms nearby, where the materials have already been assembled. Other activities will of course be carried on until they're called back.

Appropriate music can be played as the contestants exhibit their creations. Let the audience elect their "Miss America" by popular applause.

Here is a variation that has proved to be fun. Ask four girls to bring from home a dress, hat, and other accessories with which to fix up a boy as a "Miss America" candidate. Be sure the dresses are large and shapeless. Challenge the people who bring the costumes to see which one can come up with the funniest looking hat, the most outlandish earrings, the most unusual bouquet (weeds, onions, etc.). Use ridiculous names for the candidates, such as Miss Buzzard Roost, Miss Skunk Crick, Miss Monkey Mountain, and Miss Hog Woller.

When the four boys have been chosen by the audience, tell them why they have been selected and send them to rooms where the costumes have been assembled. Let each girl who brought a costume choose one other girl to help her dress up her candidate. Allow about ten minutes for this, while the audience is directed in other activities.

A Kitchen Drama
(in one messy scene)

Ask the audience to choose four men who are extra good sports. Call them to the front of the room and put an apron on each one. Uncover a church dining table on which has been placed all the necessary ingredients and utensils for making biscuits. While the audience watches, the four men make biscuits. No recipes are allowed. Each man's pan of biscuits is marked and put in the oven to bake while other activities are carried on.

When the biscuits are done, bring them out for all to see. Previously arranged judges sample and judge them. Everybody will want to get in on the "sampling," so be sure to have some butter and jelly on hand and pass the biscuits around!

A Cool Conversation

Ask the women in the group to choose the woman whom they consider to be the biggest "talker." Instruct the men to choose the fellow who can hold his own with any woman in a "gab session." Call the two representatives to the front of the room and announce that, once and for all, you're going to settle the age-old question of whether or not women can outtalk men.

Bring out of hiding a five-pound hunk of ice and tell the man that he is to hold the ice as long as the woman talks. When she pauses to take a breath, or to think of something else to say, he hands the ice to her and starts talking. So long as he continues with an unbroken stream of words, she must hold the ice. What is said does not necessarily need to make sense. It may be the quoting of nursery rhymes or the alphabet. Stop the stunt while the fun is still at a peak.

A Fashion Preview

Ask the audience to select eight of their favorite men. Call them to the front of the room and tell them that they are going to give the ladies a preview of the coming spring fashions. Place on a table or on chairs seven funny-looking, out-of-date women's hats.

While music is played, the men march around the table, hands behind their backs. When the music stops, each fellow grabs a hat, puts it on his head, and strikes a dramatic pose for the audience. The participant without a hat sits down. Remove one hat each time and continue until only one man is left.

Shadow Plays

With a tightly stretched bed sheet and a strong light behind it, a good shadow screen can be improvised. Some very humorous effects can be achieved with actors playing between the light and the sheet. The stunts can be pantomimed or lines can be spoken. Music and sound effects can add to the fun.

Some suggestions are: (1) sword-swallowing and fire-eating

act; (2) dinner table scene with bride's first biscuits; (3) dental operation with odd-shaped instruments and the extraction of a huge tooth several feet long; (4) operation with patient, doctor, huge knife, scissors, hammer, chisel, saw, large needle, etc. Doctor may withdraw many interesting and unusual objects from the patient. (Though this is old, it is always humorous, and it is amazing how many people have never seen it done.)

In doing shadow plays be sure to allow for sufficient rehearsals. The positioning of the actors and placement of the light must be carefully worked out.

The Moon Is Round

For this activity, ask the girls to choose four people to represent them—girls they feel can outsmart any boys present. Ask the boys to do likewise. Bring the eight people to the front of the room and ask them to stand facing the audience. Arrange them boy, girl, boy, girl.

Tell them that you are going to see how many can qualify to take a trip to the moon. Explain that all you ask is for each person to watch you closely and then do exactly what you do. No help from the audience, please. Stand in front of the participants with your back to the audience. Begin with the first boy and say, "Watch me, and then do exactly what I do." With your left hand, make a circular motion in the air as you say, "The moon is round." Still using your left hand, fill in two eyes, a nose, and a mouth in the imaginary circle you've drawn as you say, "It has two eyes, a nose, and a mouth." The first boy tries to repeat what you have done. He probably will do it with his right hand instead of the left. This will disqualify him and you will say, "I'm sorry, but you can't go with us to the moon."

Give the first girl a try and so on until all have tried. A few will catch on and do it correctly. Most of the audience will have caught on, too. Be sure that one player does not share the secret with his team members.

Be certain that the audience can see and hear. Elevate the players if a platform is available, and use a mike if necessary to be heard.

Hunter, Gun, Rabbit

This is an adaptation of the old game, "Rock, scissors, paper." Call up eight people to form two lines of four players each. The two lines of players stand, facing each other, on opposite sides of the platform. Each team has a captain who decides throughout the game what poses his team will assume. Each team tries to outguess the other in striking the pose of a hunter *(hands on hips)*, a gun *(position of shooting a gun)*, or a rabbit *(thumbs on temples with fingers extended)*. All three score differently in different combinations. The hunter wins over the gun because he makes the gun work; the gun wins over the rabbit because it can shoot the rabbit; the rabbit wins over the hunter because he can outrun the hunter.

To notify the players on his team what they are to represent, the captain either whispers the word "hunter," "rabbit," or "gun," to each player, or he adopts a set of finger signals which he gives his team without the other team seeing them. This can be done by standing directly in front of his team and facing them. Poses of both teams are done simultaneously when the signal "go" is given. Play until one team gets 3 points.

The Doll Shop

Call to the front the most outgoing man and woman in the group. Ask him to choose four other men to assist him while she selects four women to help her. Ask the five women and the leader of the men to stand at the front, facing the group. Announce to them that the leader of the women is the owner of a doll shop and that her four helpers are dolls.

When the "go" signal is given, the leader of the men has three minutes to try to buy a doll. His object is to make the four dolls grin or laugh—for when they do, they must sit down. The buyer asks the shopkeeper for the kind of doll he's seeking and may pick out the particular one he wants to demonstrate its abilities. He may ask a particular doll to say "Mama" or "Papa." He may ask for a soldier that can march and salute. He may ask one to skate, and so on. He can say anything funny he wishes to get the dolls tickled—but he cannot touch them. The other men are allowed to help the leader by giving him suggestions as needed. When time is called, the women who are still standing sit down and the four men take their places. The leader of the men becomes the shopkeeper, the leader of the women becomes the buyer, and the entire situation is reversed. The side with the most people left standing at the end of the allotted three minutes is the winner!

Hail, King Bo Bo

Here is a stunt that is one of the very funniest. Although many adaptations of it have been used through the years, it is still new to the majority of people in any audience.

Begin by saying that a royal king will make his appearance momentarily and that several people will get to meet him personally. Ask how many have at one time or another heard about King Bo Bo. Take those who know the trick in on the fun and get them to choose three or four girls who definitely do not know about it. Send them out of the room with a guard. Be certain that they are far enough away that they cannot see or hear.

Quickly bring to the platform a boy to be King Bo Bo. Bedspreads or sheets can be used to dress up the throne chair and also to make a robe for the King.

Borrow from the audience two large mens' class rings. Get two that are as much alike as possible. Place one on a finger of the King's left hand. Ask him to remove one shoe and sock and place the other ring on a bare toe. Be sure that the entire audience sees this. Cover up the bare foot and hide the shoe.

Ask King Bo Bo to play his part with utter seriousness. When he is all set, bring in the first victim. As she steps through the door, say, "Stop right where you are! This is the court of his Royal Highness King Bo Bo, and these (*pointing to the audience*) are the subjects of his Royal Highness. We are going to give you the unusual opportunity of becoming a member of this royal court—provided you can pass the initiation ceremony. First, you must be very serious! Please face the King and repeat after me with much feeling, 'O HAIL, KING BO BO.' " Lead the audience in applause if the candidate really made it dramatic. If not, give her a second try.

With this part of the initiation passed, bring the candidate to the platform. Ask her to kneel in front of the king. (Be sure that the throne chair is positioned so that everybody can see both the King and the person who kneels.) Ask the victim to again repeat after you two or three expressions such as, "O LIVE FOREVER, KING BO BO!" The audience applauds again if it is well done.

Now tell the candidate she has only one more test to pass and she will be a member of the Royal Court. Inform her that she must be willing to kiss the King's Royal Ring. Let her almost kiss the ring on the hand which the King is holding out and then stop her by saying, "Wait, this part of the initiation ceremony is too solemn for you to even see. You must, therefore, be blindfolded for this occasion." Although she will protest, assure her that you're not going to hurt her and go ahead and blindfold her. Be certain that she cannot possibly see. Make her place her hands behind her and let you guide her in kissing the ring. When she has finally kissed the ring, get the King to quickly conceal the hand with the ring she has just kissed and uncover his foot on which the other ring is placed. Take off the blindfold while the girl is still kneeling. If the King's knee is crossed and the foot is right where the other ring was, the poor girl will know for sure that she has kissed that big, dirty foot! Let her sit on the platform and find out what really happened as she watches the next victim.

Pillowcase Drama

This is one of the funniest things imaginable if carefully worked out. With Magic Markers, paint grotesque eyes, nose, mouth, and other face and head features on a white pillowcase. The entire pillowcase is to serve as the head of a peculiar-looking, ill-shaped creature.

When the art work is completed, ask the person who is to be the "creature" (use a girl not more than five feet tall) to put her hands upon her head so that the elbows will stick straight out on each side to fill in the corners of the pillowcase. Pull the pillowcase over the person and work with it until the painted head and face are straight. Fasten around the person's waist a cardigan sweater with all buttons fastened. Use a long sweater so that it comes within two or three inches of the floor. Stuff the sleeves with newspaper or cloth to resemble arms. You now have your "creature" completed. The fun comes when several of these are led into the room to do calisthenics or a military drill to the rhythm of a phonograph record. With the huge head, long dangling arms, and tiny short legs, it is hilariously funny!

Get Out There and Fight

During a blackout, several large boys seat themselves on a bench, backs to the audience. Their shoulders and backs are covered with a blanket so that only their heads are visible. As the light comes up, a man stands facing the fellows giving them a pep talk. The audience assumes that it is a half-time session in the dressing room at a football game. The leader must be deeply move .... men now he is counting on them as never before and that he knows they can do it! He closes his appeal by urging them to win this one for Rusty, their teammate, who is in the hospital. He is practically weeping by this time and very dramatically says, "Now, get out there and fight!"

The men jump up from the bench and go out into the audience yelling, "Peanuts, popcorn," and so on. (They walk through the audience and on out. If peanuts or popcorn will be appropriate for refreshments at whatever event you're having, why not let these fellows go ahead and pass them out?)

Fun with Tongue Twisters

A lot of fun can be had with tongue twisters. Here's one idea: Call to the front of the room two men and two women (or teenagers) who are well liked by the group. Tell the audience that you're going to settle once and for all the question as to whether or not males are sharper than females.

Hand to each person one of the following tongue twisters and give them a half minute to silently read it. Then call on each one to read his three times in succession as rapidly as possible without stopping.

1. A sifter sifting sand thrust three thousand thistles through the thick of his thumb.

2. Rubber baby buggy bumpers

3. Six long, slick, slim, slender sycamore saplings grew in the woods.

4. Nine nimble noblemen nibbling nuts

5. Five fluffy finches flying fast

6. A skunk sat on a stump. The skunk thunk the stump stunk, and the stump thunk the skunk stunk.

7. A tutor who tooted a flute tried to teach two tooters to toot. Said the two to the tutor, "Is it harder to toot, or to tutor two tooters to toot?"

8. Peter Piper picked a peck of pickled peppers. A peck of pickled peppers Peter Piper picked.

Identify That Nose

Here's a good one for young married people or any married adult group. Choose five couples and bring them to the platform. Let the men sit and the wives stand behind the chairs. Blindfold the women so that they can't possibly see. Mix the men all up so that no one is seated in front of his wife. Take the women, one at a time, and let each try to find her husband by feeling the nose of each man in the row. She is not allowed to touch any part of the face other than the nose. The leader will need to guide her hand. When she thinks she has located her husband, she makes it known and is guided to the back of his chair where she remains until all have had their turn. When all have finished, take off the blindfolds. Be sure to position the seated men in such a way that the audience can see everything that is done!

When using this with youth, call to the front several young people and their leaders and place them behind a big piece of cardboard or table paper in which small triangular holes have been cut out. (Use several strips of table paper taped together or a cardboard mattress carton from your furniture dealer. Cut the holes just large enough for a nose to stick through.)

When all are in place, let the audience, by looking at the noses, try to identify each one.

Comb Orchestra

For this activity divide the participants into groups of ten or more. Ask each group to choose a leader who is musically inclined. Hand to each group leader enough pieces of tissue paper (cut in five-inch squares) for each person in his group. Give each group ten minutes to rehearse a song of its choice to be performed for the entire group. The orchestra is to be made up of one of the most ancient instruments known to man—the comb! It is possible to achieve interesting effects by humming through the teeth of a comb which has been covered with tissue paper. The orchestra will be judged on interpretation, ensemble playing, harmony, and tone quality.

When time is called, bring the groups back together and let them perform!

Clap Rhythm

Ask each person to choose a partner and stand facing him. Then demonstrate the rhythm of slapping your thighs, clapping your hands, clapping your partner's hands with yours, and clapping your own hands again (done to a 1, 2, 3, 4 count).

When everyone has learned the rhythm, add the music, "I've Been Workin' on the Railroad," and ask the group to sing it as they do the rhythm. When this has been worked out, put two couples together with partners across from each other. One couple begins their rhythm on the count of "1" and the other couple begins on the count of "2." Be sure to get some people together and practice this activity before trying to teach it so they can help you demonstrate it.

Musical Balloon[2]

Call to the front of the room six to eight key leaders who are popular with the group. Give each one of them an uninflated balloon. Tell them that some of the world's finest music is produced with a balloon. Inflate a balloon and demonstrate the effects (noises!) that can be achieved by stretching the mouth of the balloon with both hands while permitting a little bit of air to

---

[2]Shared by Leon Mitchell, Church Recreation Department, Baptist Sunday School Board, Nashville, Tennessee.

escape. Ask the participants to inflate their balloons. Give them a minute to practice what you have demonstrated. Now tell them that they are to play a familiar melody with piano accompaniment. The pianist plays "The Blue Danube" as the balloonists create their own "music," keeping the rhythm established by the piano, of course.

To make the experience more hilarious, put a rubber band around the neck of each participant. Then pull the front side of the rubber band up over the nose. As the musicians play, they also wiggle their nose in a desperate effort to get the rubber band to move down below the nose.

Tied—Feminine Style

Call to the front of the room six girls and six boys. Ask each fellow to choose a girl and stand facing her. With hands in his pockets, the boy must tell the girl how to tie a necktie. He cannot show her how. He must keep his hands in his pockets and simply tell her how. The girl must follow his instructions and tie the necktie on her neck. When time is called, let the audience by popular applause choose the one who did the best job. Be sure to place the contestants so that the audience can see all that happens. Old-fashioned, loud-colored ties will add to the fun.

A Magician in Our Midst

People never tire of seeing tricks and trying to figure out how they were done. Here's a variation of an old one that always proves to be fun.

Choose as your helper a person whom the audience is least likely to suspect as being in on the trick. If possible, choose someone you do not know. Talk with him ahead of time to get your signals straight. Do this at a time and place where you'll not be seen. Ask your helper to sit in the audience when he arrives so that even those with whom he came will not suspect anything.

When it is time for this bit of magic, announce to the audience that you are going to share something with them that you rarely do in public. Tell them very seriously that there is somebody in the group who is possessed with unique magical abilities. Explain that it is possible that this person may not even be aware of his unusual abilities. Hold up an object (an old bottle, an unusual rock, a peculiarly-shaped stick, or just anything different looking) and give a spiel about how this object was passed down to you from your great-great-grandfather who brought it back from a trip to the East. Say that it is through the use of this object that you will be able to detect the potential magician in the room.

Walk out into the audience, letting the object lead you. A faraway look in your eyes and the muttering of some mumbo-jumbo will add atmosphere. Let the object lead you to some well-known person. Stop nearby and say, "I seem to be directed to someone in this area." Point to this individual and say, "Could it be you?" He will of course protest. Move on to two or three more people and repeat the process. Then go to your helper. He too protests but is finally persuaded to come to the front. (This must be played honestly or your secret will be betrayed.)

Take your helper to the front and place him on a platform where all can see. Pull out of a paper bag five women's hats (discarded ones from someone's attic or from a Salvation Army store. Be sure that each hat is distinctive in color and design.) Tell your helper that if he will concentrate, you're going to prove that he has powers of magic of which he has never dreamed. Place the hats on a table side by side or on five chairs where everybody can see. Tell your "magician" that you're going to touch a particular hat while his back is turned and his eyes are closed. When the audience begins to clap, he will—with his back still turned and his eyes closed—describe the hat which was touched.

Here's how it works. He takes a good look at the hats to see which one is placed third from the left as he faces them. He knows that you will touch that hat. When he turns his back, mix up the arrangement of hats remembering which one was number three. Act as if you are going to really throw him off by quietly shifting the hats. After they have been rearranged with hat number three in some other position, repeat your mumbo jumbo and with much concentration finally touch the hat that formerly was third from the left. Start the audience in applause. The "magician" concentrates very hard and then with hesitancy describes the hat that was touched. Tell him he is right! He looks shocked that it worked. Lead the audience in applause. He turns toward you during the applause and gets another look at the hats to spot number three in the present lineup. Repeat the process a time or two more and leave the audience trying to figure out how it was done.

Mind Reading[3]

Pencils and slips of paper are distributed. The player who proposes to be mind reader asks that each member of the group write a word and fold the paper in some definite way so that all are alike. A partner who is not known to the group collects them, taking care to pass in his own paper at the bottom of the pile. The mind reader presses the top paper to his forehead and says a word as though he has read it mentally. The partner promptly claims it as his own. The mind reader then unfolds the top paper as though for verification but really to discover the word to give next. Picking up the second paper he presses it to his forehead, says the word that was written on the first paper, and looks about for its claimant. Thus the reading proceeds until all the papers have been read.

[3] From *Handbook for Recreation Leaders,* U.S. Dept. of Health, Education, and Welfare. Used by permission.

Temple Reading[4]

A player leaves the room while the group selects a number. When he returns, he lays his hands over the temples of each of the players, stopping at each as if to meditate. When he does this with his partner, the partner secretly tells him the number selected by closing his teeth and relaxing, thus making the muscles in his temples move a certain number of times. He must be careful not to move his mouth and cheeks, because his method of conveying the information might then be observed.

Touch Reading[5]

A player announces that if the group will follow a certain procedure he can read names, with addresses and telephone numbers, by touching the outside of the telephone directory. He requests that some member of the group write down any number of two to four digits, add two zeros to it, subtract the original number, and state the result. Next he asks that the telephone directory be brought. He lays his hand on it a moment and pretends to meditate. Then he recites slowly a name, address, and telephone number, saying these will be found on the page indicated by that total. If the total is 18, he directs, "Look in the eighth line of the first column." If the total is 27, he says, "Look on page 27, second column, seventh line." If the total is 36, he says, "Look on page 36, third column, sixth line."

The game is based on the fact that when any number is subtracted from itself multiplied by 100 the remainder will be a figure whose digits total 9 or a multiple of 9. Therefore the player needs to memorize beforehand only three names with addresses and numbers—one on page 18 of the directory, one on page 27, and one on page 36, in the lines and columns indicated by the digits of these three numbers.

[4]*Ibid.*
[5]*Ibid.*

Magic Writing[6]

The player who claims to be a magician leaves the room, and the group chooses any word. The magician is called in, and his partner goes through the pretense of writing on the floor with a cane or stick. The scratches and flourishes he makes are of no interest to the magician, who in fact is listening to the taps his partner makes in connection with his "writing." By these the partner is spelling the chosen word. One tap means *A*, two taps mean *E*, three mean *I*, four mean *O*, and five mean *U*. He indicates the consonants by using them in their proper order for the initial words of short sentences. For example, he may spell the word "cat" in this way: He says, "Can you read this?" while he moves the stick around; next he gives one tap for the letter *A*; then he says, "This isn't easy," to indicate the letter *T*.

Four Choice[7]

A player offers to guess which of four objects placed in a row has been chosen by the group. He leaves the room or hides his eyes while the group selects one of the objects. Then his partner asks him questions which are so worded as to indicate the right answer. The number of letters in the first word of the question tells the position of the chosen object, a word of four letters meaning the fourth object, one of three meaning the third, and so on. For example, the partner may indicate the first object by saying, "I now ask you to make a choice." To indicate the second he says, "Is it this one?" For the third he says, "How about that?" For the fourth he says, "Will you choose this?" If the partner is pointing at an object not indicated by his question, the player will say that is not the one chosen. Of course the questions should not be stereotyped but should be varied continually.

[6]*Ibid.*
[7]*Ibid.*

A World Famous Magician

Announce to the audience that they are most fortunate in getting to see a world famous magician perform. After making a good spiel, bring the magician in. (Use one of your own people who is costumed, made up, and disguised. A turban will help with the disguise.) The magician carries a small bag which he places on a table where all can see.

Tell the audience that the magician speaks very little English and that much concentration will be required on their part. Tell them that he has agreed to pull a white rabbit from an empty hat, provided someone in the audience will let him borrow a hat. When nobody volunteers, point to a hat in the back of the room—or on some woman's head and ask if that hat can be used. The owner will naturally protest but finally agree. (This has been worked out ahead so that the hat to be used is not a good one.) Ask two people to come forward to hold the hat. Be sure that they stand where the magician can be seen.

From the bag, the magician takes a pint jar of flour and pours it into the hat. Of course the person who owns the hat must react each time something is poured into it. Other ingredients are brought out of the bag and ceremoniously dumped into the hat. With eyes closed, the magician mutters some mumbo jumbo. He opens his eyes to find that nothing has happened. He stirs the mixture vigorously and repeats the closed-eyes ceremony. Again, nothing happens. He discovers what is wrong. He has left out an important ingredient. He takes from his bag two raw eggs, breaks them, and dramatically lets them fall into the mixture in the hat. With much confidence, he stirs the contents of the hat with a big spoon and repeats his mumbo jumbo routine. Again, nothing happens. He makes a final try by bringing from his bag a carton or pint of milk which he pours into the hat. The mumbo jumbo is repeated in melodramatic manner, but all to no avail. He looks helplessly at the two men holding the hat and says, "Someone in the room not concentrate! Cannot produce rabbit!

Please give hat back to nice man." The two helpers carry the hat to the owner who acts quite upset as he takes the hat and walks out of the room. He must be careful to not overplay his role. The audience must not know that he is in on the trick!

Choose the magician with much care. He needs to be someone with ability to pantomime the ideas he feels but cannot speak.

Bottle Orchestra
Clyde Maguire

Someone who knows music will have to prepare the bottles used in the orchestra. Sit at a piano and "tune" ten soft-drink bottles from middle C up to E on the C scale. This is done by filling the bottles with water to varying heights. It is not hard to do, but takes a little time. As you press each bottle against your lower lip and blow across it, you will blow a different note. The notes are raised or lowered by increasing or decreasing the amount of water.

The orchestra will have to rehearse. They may play "Mary Had a Little Lamb," "Dixie," or any other familiar tune.

The emcee gives the orchestra a big introduction. The ten members and the conductor all wear white, with colored sashes about their waists. The conductor has a baton in his hand and directs by pointing at the member who is to blow the next note. With a bit of practice this makes a most entertaining feature.

"Country Gardens" Rhythm
Clyde Maguire

As all are seated at the table, give instructions. Guests are to beat rhythm as pianist plays the old English folk tune "Country Gardens."

On the first eight beats, guests, holding fork in left hand, strike table eight times.

On the second eight beats, guests, holding knife in right hand, strike table eight times.

On the third eight beats, guests, holding knife and fork, strike them together eight times.

On the fourth eight beats, guests, holding knife in right hand, strike glass eight times.

Then repeat all four actions on the last thirty-two beats. This is always an entertaining feature.

Easter Hat Show

Divide the participants into small groups and give each a stack of old newspapers, scissors, pins, scraps of crepe paper, yarn, ribbon, and other odds and ends. Each group has fifteen minutes to create the most outlandish hat they can imagine. Allow two entries from each group.

When time is called, ask the chosen models to parade back and forth across the front of the room so that all can see. Choose a first- and second-place winner. If possible, make color slides of all the models. The slides can be a lot of fun at a later time.

The Mysterious Echo

Here is an old favorite that has been done in many different ways. Tell the group that there is something very strange about this particular spot (the place where this stunt is being performed). For years, there has been at certain times of the day a mysterious echo that nobody has been able to explain. Tell the group that you're going to see if the echo can be clearly heard and understood today. Of course, it will be necessary for each person in the audience to concentrate if the mysterious echo is to be heard.

When the right atmosphere has been created, say, "Hello-oh," and wait expectantly for the echo. It comes from off in the distance and is an exact echo of what was said. Other words and sentences are echoed in the same manner. Then say, "The girls in our group are the very greatest!" The echo comes again. Then use the name of a favorite in the group and say, "Jim Jones is the smartest, most talented man we know." The echo comes back with one word—"Baloney."

The stunt is performed by use of a confederate who is hidden down a hallway or in an adjoining room. When the stunt is done in a camp setting, the possibilities of the echo effect are unlimited.

Blind Banana Feed

This is an old stunt but is always very funny. Bring three or four couples to the platform. Blindfold each person so that he can't possibly see. Fasten a towel or a plastic bag from the cleaners around each person's neck to protect his clothing. Give each one a banana. When the signal is given, each person simultaneously feeds his partner. This means that each individual is eating and at the same time feeding his partner. The couple finishing first is the winner.

Papa Shot a Bear

Call to the front of the room eight or ten young people everybody likes. Tell them that they are going to have the privilege of reliving with you a bear hunt you enjoyed with your dad when you were a young boy. Line the people up, shoulder to shoulder, and ask them to repeat everything you say and do.

"One day Papa took me bear hunting." (*All repeat.*) "I was just that high." (*Measure height with hand and all do the same.*) "We were walking through a dense forest." (*All lift feet and walk in place.*) "When suddenly Papa stopped." (*All repeat.*) "He squatted down." (*All get down.*) "He put his rifle against his shoulder and aimed." (*All pantomime holding the rifle.*) "And I said, 'Papa, where's the bear?' And he said 'Over there.'" (*At this point, the leader quickly bumps the person to his left and the entire row topples over like dominoes—one knocking the other down.)*

Dress That Mannequin

Divide the participants into several small groups of not more than ten people. Assign each group to a room nearby where newspapers, crepe paper, scraps of ribbon, scissors, Scotch tape, etc., are available. Allow each group fifteen minutes to fix up two men or boys as mannequins in a department store window. One is to be dressed in a wedding gown and the other in a formal. Each group is responsible for dressing and posing the two mannequins. When time is called, ask each group to bring the mannequins to the platform and pose them. Let three judges choose the first- and second-place winners.

(When using this activity with large crowds, choose four popular men or boys and send them to nearby rooms where girls fix them up while other activities are carried on with the group.)

Blind Art

Choose four popular couples for this activity. Bring them to the front of the room and place a large paper bag over the head of each one. Give each couple a black Magic Marker. When the "go" signal is given, each man with the sack still over his head draws eyes, nose, and other features on the front of his partner's sack. Give them three minutes. When time is called, the women have their turn. Let the audience by popular applause choose the best art work.

(When this activity is used for small groups, all guests participate.)

Fake Fortune-telling

People are always eager to see a trick pulled on one of their favorite friends. Here is a good one! Announce to the group that you have asked a world famous fortune-teller to demonstrate her abilities for the group. Ask the people in the audience to choose a girl and a boy whose future they would like to have foretold. Send the two victims out of the room. Quickly costume one of the girls you have already selected and worked with. A colorful sheet draped around her and a shawl on the head will do. Some showy beads fastened around the head will add to the costume. With a burning candle, black the bottom of a plate or cereal bowl. Be sure that the audience is aware of this. Pour water into the plate or bowl when the bottom has been thoroughly blacked. Ask the "fortune-teller" to hold the dish with one hand for the ceremony to follow.

Bring in the first victim and place him in front of the "fortune-teller." Be sure to position them so the audience can see. She calls attention to the plate—handed down to her from her great-great-grandmother who toured every country in the world with her unique fortune-telling abilities. It is through the dish that the wonderful impressions come.

She reminds the victim that he is to look her squarely in the eyes at all times and concentrate. She then looks into the dish of water, rubs her fingers under the bottom, does some mumbo jumbo, and feels of the victim's forehead. As she does so, she says in a mysterious voice, "I see riches in your future." Of course the fingers leave a black smudge on the person's forehead. The process is repeated with other things foretold. She finishes by telling the victim that she has for him a magic mirror which will give him a look into the future. He takes the mirror and, of course, sees his blackened forehead, cheeks, and nose. He gets to watch the second victim.

CHAPTER THREE

PREPARED SKITS

Can'tsee Poorsight

Here is a delightful skit that offers unlimited possibilities for creative fun. It is in outline form and can be developed as elaborately or simply as desired.

Characters

Can'tsee Poorsight
Hornrim
Can'tsee's sister

Plot

As the scene opens, Can'tsee and her sister are discussing Hornrim who has been invited over for dinner. Can'tsee can only think of how handsome Hornrim is—and the fact that he is to be her date for the evening. The sister tells Can'tsee that she thinks it unfair of her to fool poor Hornrim. Can'tsee is as blind as a bat without her glasses but is afraid Hornrim will not like her if he sees her wearing them. Therefore, she has decided to "operate" without her glasses.

While the sisters are discussing the deceptive plan, there is a knock at the door. (This is all done in pantomime so the audience can see both Hornrim and Can'tsee.) Can'tsee, all in a dither, takes a final look around the room to get a mental picture of things and then pulls off her glasses and puts them in her pocket.

Hornrim takes a careful look at the doorknob—gets it fixed in his mind—and then pockets his glasses. He squints as the door opens and Can'tsee greets him. She squints at him and introduces her sister. He acknowledges the introduction by shaking the sleeve of a coat hanging on a coatrack.

The sister excuses herself and exits.

The hilarity builds as they try to act "natural" without their *very eyes*. Hornrim misses the divan when he sits. Can'tsee shows him pictures from a photograph album. Most of them are upside down—but he doesn't know it. (Be sure the audience can see that they are upside down!) She shows him one which she says is her sister. It is a large picture of a dog. He says, "Oh, she is beautiful. She looks just like you." Can'tsee is flattered no end! Finally, she serves him dinner. She excuses herself and fixes the table (a folding table will work fine)—we see her slip on her glasses as she turns her back to him. She places him at the table and while she is in the kitchen, he puts on his glasses long enough to get the lay of the land. When Can'tsee returns, she decides to change the place she wants him to sit. He insists that this is a perfectly comfortable place, but she changes him anyway. He tucks the corner of the tablecloth (a big towel which he brags on and which Can'tsee says is her best Irish linen) under his belt. (Be sure the audience sees this so they can more fully appreciate the climactic moment.)

The peak of fun is reached when she serves him apple pie. She asks if he likes whipped cream on his pie. He says he just loves it. She gets the dispenser (shaving cream) and says, "Tell me when." Can'tsee of course misses the pie and sprays Hornrim's face! He yells, "When," and jumps up. The towel he has tucked under his belt pulls everything off the table. (Use plastic dishes or some that are no good.)

Both characters exit immediately. Can'tsee is crying of course.

The success of this piece depends upon the creativity of the two main characters and their ability to pantomime the situations involved.

The Stand-in

This skit has been successfully presented in camps, church socials, high schools, civic clubs, and many other places. It offers an outline which can be developed as elaborately or simply as desired.

Characters

Ronnie Boy, the tall, handsome "star" of the production
Dolores Darling, the gay-nineties-type heroine of the show
First Cowpoke, a rough cowhand
Second Cowpoke, another rough cowhand
The Director, a movie director type, fully equipped with dark glasses, megaphone, script, his personal chair, etc.
The Stand-in, an eager young actor who is willing to do almost anything to be a success
Extras. Several other people can be worked in as cameramen, light and sound engineers, property crew, etc.

Setting

A typical movie studio with a "set" for a western "horse opera": piano, table, and chairs. Because of the use of water, this skit should be done outside when possible. Otherwise be sure to have a crew with mops prepared to clean up the mess.

The Story

The western is being filmed and the "star," Ronnie Boy, must have a stand-in to take all the dirty jobs. In each scene, just when the star is about to get in trouble, the Stand-in has to take the beating.

Scene 1:

Dolores is standing by the piano and the two rough cowhands

are talking to her. RONNIE BOY steps in and is about to get beaten up when the DIRECTOR screams, "Cut!" The STAND-IN is brought forward and put in the scene to replace RONNIE BOY. The DIRECTOR then yells, "Roll'em!" The STAND-IN takes the beating!

Scene 2:

RONNIE BOY crawls across the desert and comes to two cowhands. He is dying of thirst and begs them for water. They pick up a bucket of water and start to throw it in his face, when the DIRECTOR yells, "Cut!" The STAND-IN is again brought in and the water is dumped on him.

Scene 3:

RONNIE BOY approaches the cowhands of Scene 1 and says he hears they have been seeing DOLORES after *he* beat *them* up the other day. One of the cowhands picks up a pie from the table and starts to mash it in Ronnie Boy's face while the other cowhand holds him. The DIRECTOR says, "Cut," and brings in the STAND-IN. As the pie is pushed, the STAND-IN ducks, and the man holding him gets it.

Scene 4:

DOLORES is standing by the piano for the final love scene. RONNIE BOY comes in. He hesitates, struck by his love for her. They move toward each other and prepare to embrace. Just before they reach each other, the STAND-IN jumps up and yells, "Cut!" He pushes RONNIE BOY aside and embraces DOLORES. Quick blackout or curtain.

The more ham included in this skit the better. The camera can be made from a cardboard box, painted black. Be sure to have at least a couple of good rehearsals. The timing is real important. The cowpoke who gets the pie in the face should be a good sport who is loved by the people who will be in the audience.

The Fatal Quest
(a 10-minute drama in three acts)

Here is another favorite that is sure to go over if well done.

It can be presented in pantomime while a good reader reads the script, or it can be done with each character reading his own lines. It is ridiculously funny if the characters also read the stage directions as part of their lines. Of course appropriate actions will be necessary along with the lines.

Characters

The King	The Lovely Princess
The Devoted Queen	The Curtains
The Handsome Duke	The Kitten

Act I

CURTAIN:	The Curtain rises for the first act.
KING:	Enter the King
QUEEN:	Followed by the devoted Queen.
KING:	He seats himself on his throne, his scepter in hand.
QUEEN:	The Queen stands gracefully beside him, gazing at him fondly. "My Lord," she says in gentle tones, "why do we keep the Princess hidden from the eyes of men? Will wedlock never be hers?"
KING:	The King waxes stern. "Fair Queen," he says gruffly, "a thousand times have I repeated—the Princess shall become the wife of no man."
DUKE:	Enter the handsome Duke. "O King," he says in manly tones, "I have this morning come from your majestic borders. I have a message of greatest importance."
PRINCESS:	The Princess enters at left. At the sight of the handsome Duke, she is startled. Her embarrassment

FUN WITH PREPARED SKITS/CHAPTER 3

	increases her loveliness.
DUKE:	At first glance the Duke falls madly in love.
KING:	The King arises in excitement. "Speak," he shouts at the Duke, "and be gone!"
DUKE:	The Duke gazes at the Princess, his message forgotten.
PRINCESS:	The lovely maiden blushes and drops her eyes.
QUEEN:	"Daughter," says the Queen, "why do you intrude yourself here without permission?"
PRINCESS:	The Princess opens her mouth to speak.
DUKE:	The Duke holds his breath.
PRINCESS:	"Alas," says the maiden in tones melting with sweetness, "my Angora kitten has strayed away and is lost."
DUKE:	"Fair Princess," cries the Duke in tones filled with feeling, "service for you were joy. The kitten I swear to find." With high courage he strides away.
KING:	"Stop him! Stop him!" shouts the King fiercely. "My servants shall find the cat for the Princess." Exit the King.
QUEEN:	Followed by the devoted Queen.
CURTAIN:	The Curtain falls.

Act II

CURTAIN:	The Curtain rises for the second act.
PRINCESS:	The fair Princess stands at the window. She hears the distant sound of hoofs. "It is he," she cries, placing her hand upon her beating heart.
KING:	Enter the King.
QUEEN:	Followed by the devoted Queen.
DUKE:	The Duke steps in buoyantly, Puss in arms.
PRINCESS:	"My kitten, my kitten," cries the Princess joyously. She takes her pet in her arms, but her eyes follow the stalwart form of the Duke.
KING:	The King is pierced with jealousy.

Duke:	The Duke falls upon his knees before the King. "O King," he says manfully, "I have found the kitten! I have come to claim the reward, the hand of the Princess."
King:	The King trembles with wrath. "Be gone!" he shouts furiously. "The hand of the Princess shall be won by no cat."
Duke:	The Duke departs. As he passes the Princess, he grasps her soft hand. "I will return," he whispers in her ear.
Princess:	The Princess does not speak, but her clear blue eyes reflect the secret of her soul.
Curtain:	The Curtain falls.

Act III

Curtain:	The Curtain rises for the third and fatal act.
King:	The King stands morosely in the center of the stage.
Queen:	The Queen stands sadly beside him. "My Lord," she says in pleading tones, "relent. The Princess weeps day and night, nor will she be comforted."
King:	The King turns his back. "Hold your peace!" he says in harsh tones.
Queen:	The Queen weeps.
Duke:	Enter the Duke, his sword at his side. "O King," he says in a white passion, "for the last time I ask you for the hand of your daughter."
King:	The King spurns him. "Be gone!" he shouts once more.
Duke:	The Duke draws his sword and stabs the King.
King:	The King gasps and dies.
Queen:	"My Lord, my Lord," cries the Queen passionately, and she falls dead upon the King.
Duke:	"Great Caesar's Ghost, what have I done!" cries the Duke in anguish. He drinks a cup of poison and falls dead.

FUN WITH PREPARED SKITS/CHAPTER 3

PRINCESS: Hearing the cry, the Princess enters. She stops, transfixed at the horrible sight before her. "Heaven help me," she cries, waving her shapely arms. "I die of grief." She falls dead upon the breast of her beloved.
KING: Woe, woe, the King of the land is dead.
QUEEN: Alas, alas, the devoted Queen is dead.
PRINCESS: The Princess is dead, and beautiful even in death.
CURTAIN: The Curtain falls.

Postlude

CURTAIN: The Curtain rises for the Postlude.
KING: The King is dead.
QUEEN: The devoted Queen is still dead.
DUKE: The manly Duke is still dead.
PRINCESS: The beautiful Princess is still dead and still beloved.
CURTAIN: The Curtain falls forever.

"Fun with Hamlet and His Friends"
(Adapted for second-graders)

(This clever monologue is to be read as a second-grader would do it. Use a large encyclopedia covered to represent a second-grade reader. The humor comes both through the lines and the childish manner in which the piece is read.)

See the man. What a funny man. His name is Hamlet. He is a prince. He is sad. "Why are you sad, Hamlet?"

"I am sad for my father has died," says Hamlet.

See Hamlet run. Run, Hamlet, run.

On the way to the castle, he meets a ghost.

"Where are you going?" asks the ghost.

"I am going to the castle," says Hamlet.

"Boo! Boo!" says the ghost.

"What is your name, you silly ghost?" asks Hamlet, clapping his hands.

"I am your father," says the ghost. "I was a good king. Uncle Claudius is a bad king. He gave me poison. Would you like poison?"

"Oh, no," says Hamlet. "I would not like poison."

"Will you avenge me, Hamlet?" asks the ghost.

"Oh, yes," says Hamlet. "I will avenge you. What fun it will be to avenge you."

See Hamlet run. Run, Hamlet, run.

On the way he meets a girl.

"Where are you going?" asks the girl.

"I am going to the castle," says Hamlet. "What is your name?"

"My name is Ophelia."

"Why are you laughing?" asks Hamlet. "You are a silly goose."

"I laugh because you are so funny," says Ophelia. "I laugh because you are a schizophrenic. Are you not a schizophrenic?"

"I am not a schizophrenic. I pretend, for I want to fool my uncle. What fun it is to pretend I am a schizophrenic!"

See Hamlet run. Run, Hamlet, run!

Hamlet is going to his mother's room.

"I have something to tell you, Mother," says Hamlet. "He is hiding behind the curtain. Why is he hiding behind the curtain? I shall stab him. What fun it will be to stab him through the curtain."

See Hamlet draw his sword. See Hamlet stab. Stab, Hamlet, stab.

See Uncle Claudius' blood. See Uncle Claudius' blood gush. Gush, blood, gush.

See Uncle Claudius fall. How funny he looks, stabbed. Ha, ha, ha!

But it is not Uncle Claudius. It is Polonius. Polonius is Ophelia's father.

FUN WITH PREPARED SKITS/CHAPTER 3

What fun Hamlet is having.

"You are naughty, Hamlet," says Hamlet's mother. "You have stabbed Polonius."

But Hamlet's mother is not cross. She does not tell Hamlet to go play in the traffic, nor does she take his sword away from him, for she loves Hamlet. He is a good boy. And Hamlet loves his mother. She is a good mother. Hamlet loves his mother very much. Hamlet loves his mother very, very much.

Perhaps Hamlet loves his mother a little too much?

See Hamlet run. Run, Hamlet, run.

"Where are you going," asks a man.

"I am going to find Uncle Claudius," says Hamlet. "What is your name?"

"My name is Macbeth," says the man.

"Oh, I am sorry," says Hamlet, "but I am afraid you are in the wrong play. Your play does not open in this theater until next week."

"Oh, I am so embarrassed," says Macbeth, running quickly away.

"It will happen," says Hamlet.

On the way to the castle, Hamlet passes a brook. In the brook he sees Ophelia. Ophelia is drowning. Hamlet does not know why she is drowning. He thinks perhaps it is because she is in the brook.

"Where are you going?" asks Ophelia.

"I am going to find Uncle Claudius. Why are you drowning, Ophelia?" asks Hamlet.

"Blub, blub," says Ophelia.

"Oh," says Hamlet, as he starts on down the road.

See Hamlet run. Run, Hamlet, run.

On the way he meets a man.

"Where are you going?" asks the man.

"Oh, oh. I am Laertes," says the man. "Let us draw swords. Let us duel!"

"I don't think I am going to find Uncle Claudius," says Hamlet.

See Hamlet and Laertes duel. See Laertes stab Hamlet. See Hamlet's mother drink poison.

See Hamlet stab King Claudius. See everybody wounded. See everybody bleeding. See everybody dying. See everybody dead. What fun they are having.

Now, wouldn't you like to play that?

"Henry"[1]

This humorous monologue deals with the "tragic" tale of Henry as told by his bashful girl friend. It can be done by either male or female.

Although a complete costume is by no means essential, the following touches will add to the fun:
> a blond wig or a new mophead for hair
> front teeth blacked out with tooth enamel
> artificial nose and black horn-rimmed glasses

(All of these items can be secured in trick shops.)

The Story

I would like to tell you about my boyfriend, Henry. One day, Henry and I were walking down the railroad tracks *(giggle)* holding hands *(pretend you're holding Henry's hand)*.

We were having so much fun . . . just Henry *(point toward Henry by your side)* and me *(point toward yourself)*.

All of a sudden, we heard a noise *(cup your hands over your mouth and make a faraway, soft sound of a train whistle and look frightened)* and I turned to Henry and I said, "Henry, what is that

---

[1]This version of "Henry" and the following version of "Peanut Butter" were shared by Robert Brooks, Exchange Avenue Baptist Church, Oklahoma City, Oklahoma.

noise?" And he said, "I dunno!" *(The "I dunno" is done in a "dumb" fashion.)*

So, we just walked down the railroad tracks some more . . . holding hands . . . and we were having so much fun . . . just Henry and me. And all of a sudden, we heard the noise again. *(Repeat the train whistle a bit louder.)* I turned to Henry and said, "Henry, what is that noise?" And he said, "I dunno!"

(Repeat the same thing a couple more times with the train getting a little closer and louder each time. The fourth train whistle should be loud enough to fill the room. Then the concluding lines are given.)

I turned to Henry and I said . . . but Henry wasn't there. *(Sob and cry as you see the awful sight. Then move to various places near the speaking area to pick up the pieces.)*

Over here was a leg!

And over here was an arm!

Over here was another leg!

Over here was his body!

And over here was his head!

(Look at all the pieces of his body in your outstretched arms.)

I held him in my arms, and I said, "Henry, pull yourself together!"

"Peanut Butter"

"Peanut Butter" is a lot of fun to tell. Start off as if your mouth is full of peanut butter. This effect can easily be created by curling the tongue up and back, pressing it to the roof of the mouth. Of course, the words will need to be exaggerated and made clearly understandable. Much of the success of this piece will depend upon humorous gestures.

The Story

There are three ways to get peanut butter out of the roof of your mouth. One way is to swallow it. *(Swallow hard, making the pantomime bold enough to be seen by everybody.)* But that doesn't always work.

Another way to get peanut butter out of your mouth is to blow it out. *(Pantomime this action in exaggerated manner.)* But that doesn't always work.

The other way is to scrape it out with the end of your finger. *(Laboriously scrape it out and hold it on the end of your finger. Then talk in a normal voice since the peanut butter is out.)*

There are three ways to get peanut butter off the end of your finger. One way is to blow it off. *(Make a real effort to blow it off.)* But that doesn't always work.

Another way to get peanut butter off the end of your finger is to shake it off. *(Try desperately to shake the peanut butter off. Some of it flies off and lands on your clothes.)* But that is too messy. *(Wipe off the side of your leg.)*

The other way to get peanut butter off the end of your finger is to lick it off. *(Place finger back in your mouth and lick the peanut butter off. Now you're back where you started with the mouth full again.)*

Now, there are three ways to get peanut butter out of the roof of your mouth.

"Pure White" *(pronounced p-yore)*

(This monologue is to be given in a very serious manner with a deadpan face and voice. The fun of the piece will be intensified if the person doing the monologue is dressed in a white sheet or gown and carries a white lily. The face should be whitened with starch or flour. Use a "hillbilly" accent and a "nasal twang.")

I have come to tell you the great and glorious history of that great and radiant character, Adelaide. *(Pronounced Ah-da-laid)* Adelaide was born. (You mothers know what I mean.) And when she was born they put a p-yore white diaper on her and dressed her in a p-yore white gown and on her feet they put p-yore white bootees—so symbolic of the life she would lead.

As time went by they began to feed her p-yore white Cream of Wheat with p-yore white sugar and p-yore white milk on it—so symbolic of the life she would lead.

As time went by, Adelaide began to think about what she would like to be. She couldn't be a pianist because of the black keys, and she couldn't be a sec-re-tary because of the black typewriter ribbon. So she decided she would be a nurse—because then she could drape herself in p-yore white from head to toe—so symbolic of the life she would lead.

As time went by, Adelaide became a nurse and was sent to surgery. Ah—and there she met Horace—an intern clothed in p-yore white—a p-yore white scrub cap, a p-yore white scrub suit and p-yore white shoes—so symbolic of the life he would lead.

As time went by, Horace asked Adelaide for a date, and he took her to a drugstore and bought her a p-yore white vanilla milkshake and ordered for himself a p-yore white marshmallow sundae—so symbolic of the life he would lead.

As time went by Horace and Adelaide were married in a p-yore white church, dressed in p-yore white cl-othes, and Adelaide carried p-yore white roses—so symbolic of the life they would lead.

As time went by—alas, alas, one evening Horace came home from work, he found Adelaide sitting in a chair—her face p-yore white—and she was knitting a p-yore white bootee—SO SYMBOLIC!

The Lover's Errand

(Here is a delightful skit from the early 1900's. It is hilariously funny if costuming and characterizations are done in keeping with the period.)

Characters

Harold, a straightforward youth with roundabout methods
Daisy, a very simple maiden

Scene

The living room at Daisy's. A sofa or two chairs placed down right are the necessary properties. Daisy, wearing a gingham dress, is dusting and singing. There is a knock at the door, left, and she goes to admit Harold, an awkward country boy with a large straw hat and a coat too large for him. Daisy is very coy; Harold, very bashful.

DAISY: Oh, hello, Harold. Did you come to see me?

HAROLD: No, I mean, yes,—that is, I just came over to ask you somethin'.

DAISY: O-o-oh, Harold! Come over and sit down here on the sofa. *(They sit down.)*

HAROLD: I—I just got a minute. I—I got to ask you about somethin'. You see Mother—she—

DAISY: *(sentimentally):* Yes, Harold, I understand. I always did like your mother.

HAROLD: That so?

DAISY: *(demurely):* Yes, that's nice. Isn't it?

HAROLD: *(baffled):* W-e-e-ll, I dunno. *(with animation)* Say, you see where Jim Hawkins' barn burnt down last week? Gee, I wisht I hadn't a' missed that there fire! Ain't often we get so much excitement around Beanville.

DAISY: *(moving closer):* Now, Harold, you didn't come over to tell me about the fire.

HAROLD (*admiringly*): Gee, Daisy, how'd you know that?
DAISY: A woman's understandin' I guess.
HAROLD: Sounds more like mind-reading to me.
DAISY (*moving closer as Harold squeezes himself into his corner*): Now, Harold, you ain't afraid to speak up, are you?
HAROLD: Say, guess you didn't hear me speak up in experience meetin' last week, did you? Parson said I was gettin' right good at speakin' up!
DAISY (*moving closer*): I—I'd like to hear you speak up right now, Harold.
HAROLD (*somewhat perplexed*): Don't seem like this here's the proper time or place, Daisy.
DAISY: W-e-ll, Pa's out in the barn, and Ma's gone down the road a piece. There ain't no one here but you and me, Harold.
HAROLD: No, I couldn't speak up here nohow. 'Tain't the same. You come around to meetin' next week. Then I will. (DAISY *plumps herself down on other end of sofa and pouts. Harold looks at her in dumb surprise.*) Now you ain't mad at me, Daisy?
DAISY: Well, ain't you goin' to tell me what you came for, Harold?
HAROLD: W-e-ll, I got somethin' to ask you.
DAISY: Y-e-es?
HAROLD: Maybe I better wait and ask your ma.
DAISY: Oh, Ma don't care.
HAROLD: Sakes alive, I wisht it was over with!
DAISY: A-a-aw, Harold! That ain't a nice way to talk.
HAROLD: Well, I got the milkin' to do and drive Jerusha down to the blacksmith's. Beats all, the way she throws her shoes.
DAISY: Guess you don't think I've got anything to do but sit here.

HAROLD: Well, I might just as well ask you and get it over with.
DAISY *(a-flutter with expectation):* Yes, Harold. Go right ahead. I'm listenin'.
HAROLD *(getting up and going toward the door):* Guess—guess some other time'll do jest as well. Guess I might as well be gettin' along home.
DAISY *(going over to him):* You jest ain't got spunk enough to ask me, that is what.
HAROLD *(desperately):* Well, I'm goin' to ask—I'm goin' to ask you right now. Mother sez for me to ask you, kin she borry your petticoat pattern!
DAISY *(furious and disappointed): Yes,* she kin have it and don't you ever come sneakin' around in here askin' me any more questions, Harold Jenkins. I never want to see you again! *(She flounces out, right)*
HAROLD: I sure feel sorry for the feller who marries *her!*

The Russian Quartet[2]

This skit requires five men or boys. Choose the largest person you can find to play the role of quartet director. Three of the other characters should be people of average size. The fourth should be the smallest man or boy available.

Makeup and costumes (bathrobes, etc.) will add atmosphere.

The leader enters and in broken English expresses his delight in being able to share the quartet with the United States, as well as the other countries of the world. He introduces the quartet one at a time with the smallest person entering last. Russian names can be given to each person to add to the fun.

---

[2] This version was shared by Joe Mason, First Baptist Church, Nashville, Tennessee.

When the quartet has been properly introduced, the leader stands facing them, dramatically lifts his baton, and starts directing them. After singing or humming a few measures of a familiar melody, one member of the quartet starts making peculiar squeaks and sounds and singing off-key. The director is obviously upset and stops the music. He takes one of the singers outside. The audience hears a terrible commotion (screams, yells, banging sounds, etc.). When the noise subsides, the leader reenters without his cohort.

The director looks the remaining trio over and once again raises his baton and starts the music. A second person gets off and discordant sounds result. This person is taken from the room and is given the same treatment the first one received.

The conductor returns and the process is repeated with the third member of the quartet being taken from the room. When the leader returns, he faces the remaining quartet member, the smallest one in the group. The baton once again lifts and the lone singer sings hopelessly off-key. The director picks him up and carries him out. The audience once again hears the commotion. The noise comes to an abrupt end. There is a moment of tense silence—and then the door opens and in walks the smallest member of the quartet, brushing off his hands!

Sofapillio

Here is a favorite that has delighted old and young alike. It can be done as a memorized performance, pantomimed by the characters as a reader dramatically reads the script, or each character can hold a script and read his own lines. Regardless of which approach is used, sufficient rehearsals will need to be scheduled to get it adequately prepared.

Characters

RUDEBAGIO and SPAGHETTIO: In love with Sofapillio
SWEEP UPPIO and SAPOLIO: Maids of Sofapillio
SOFAPILLIO: The heroine

Introduction

(all characters enter)

SPAGHETTIO: I am Spaghettio, I love Sofapillio
But me she'll not havio, for she loves Rudebagio.
RUDEBAGIO: I am Rudebagio, I love Sofapillio
And her will I marrio to spite old Spaghettio.
SWEEP UPPIO: *(carries broom)*:
I am Sweep Uppio, the maid of Sofapillio;
The friend of Spaghettio, the foe of Rudebagio.
SAPOLIO: *(carries brush)*:
I am Sapolio, the maid of Sofapillio;
But I do not likio the way she does actio!
SOFAPILLIO: *(surrounded by pillows)*:
I am Sofapillio. I don't know what to doio,
For two men do fightio to win my lovio.

(all characters exit except Sapolio and Sweep Uppio)

Scene 1

SAPOLIO: Ho there, Sweep Uppio! What is the last reportio of the love affairio of Sofapillio?
SWEEP UPPIO: Oh, it is worse than everio! It's enough to make one sweario,
That she keeps Spaghettio on the jumpio.
SAPOLIO: Oh, but she is a flirtio, but I know what I'll doio!
I'll go and help Spaghettio, for I hate Rudebagio,
Because he got my floor dirtio which I had just washed upio.
SWEEP UPPIO: Good for you, Sapolio, and I too will helpio
Every bit I canio to stop Rudebagio from win-

	ning Sofapillio,
	For I just cannot standio the way she does actio.
SAPOLIO:	Look, here comes Rudebagio. Let's get behind this bushio
	And see what she doesio, then go and tell Spaghettio.
	(enter Sofapillio and Rudebagio)
SOFAPILLIO:	Oh, it is you, Rudebagio? My heart it went thumpio
	For fear it was Spaghettio. You know how I feario
	To tell him that my lovio has gone from him to youio.
RUDEBAGIO:	My sweet Sofapillio! Be it ever my endeavorio
	To spare you any painio, but why not this avoidio
	And with me elopio in my little Fordio
	And to some preacher goio?
	And we'll wedio this very nightio:
	Then we'll take a tripio and to our home we'll goio
	You as my wifio, my dear Sofapillio.
SOFAPILLIO:	My clever Rudebagio! Of all the rash thingsio
	I ever heardio, this is the worstio!
	But it does temptio my spirit of adventurio
	And I will sure be readio to go with youio
	This very same nightio when the moon comes upio.
RUDEBAGIO:	My brave Sofapillio! You have saved my lifio,
	For I was getting desperatio in my love for youio,
	My dear Sofapillio. But I must awayio
	And get the Fordio readio for our grand flightio,
	Farewell, my sweet girlio! *(Kisses her hand and waves farewell. As Rudebagio leaves, Sofapillio*

FUN WITH PREPARED SKITS/CHAPTER 3

goes into the house, and the maids come out.)

SWEEP UPPIO: I am sure it was worthio the cramp in my legio
For sitting so stiffio behind that old bushio
To hear that grand plotio for that wild escapio.

SAPOLIO: And I, too, agreeio, that it was worthio—
But we must awayio to tell Spaghettio.

SWEEP UPPIO: Oh, there's no needio, for here he does comeio.
Say, do you knowio that old Rudebagio
And sweet Sofapillio are going to elopio
In the little Fordio, this very same nightio—
And they're going to wedio?

SPAGHETTIO: This is not truio, for sweet Sofapillio
Is my betrothedio. How come you by this newsio?

SAPOLIO: We heard it just nowio behind this bushio,
And we say as they plannedio that they would elopio.

SPAGHETTIO: That blankety-blank Rudebagio! I'll get his goatio,
I'll make him payio! I'll spoil his schemio!
I'll make him deadio!
But thanks for the newsio. And now I must goio.

(All leave.)

Scene 2

(Spaghettio and maids come in looking for a hiding place.)

SPAGHETTIO: We'll hide hereio. Hark, here he comesio.
(They hide and Rudebagio comes in.)

RUDEBAGIO: Come, Sofapillio. The time is now hereio for us to elopio.
(Sofapillio comes in, if possible as through a window.)

SOFAPILLIO: Oh, Rudebagio, I cannot goio! I'm so scaredio!

RUDEBAGIO: Hark, what is thatio? Ah, it's Spaghettio!

	(Spaghettio and maids come from their hiding place.)
SPAGHETTIO:	I've got you, Rudebagio! I'll make you deadio. We'll have a duelio with our stilettio.
	(They fight, while Sofapillio runs around screaming. Finally both men fall dead.)
SOFAPILLIO	*(on knees):*
	My heart is brokeio. I, too, shall dieio. For one of my griefio cannot liveio. Alas, I am deadio! *(Falls dead over Rudebagio.)*
SAPOLIO	*(hitting herself on the head with a spoon, falls dead):*
	Alas, I am deadio!
SWEEP UPPIO	*(falls dead):*
	Alas, I, too, am deadio!

An Interview with Punchy McPugg[3]

This skit involves two men or boys. One acts as the sportscaster who interviews the world-renowned boxer, and the other plays the role of the boxer, Punchy McPugg.

Dress the boxer for the part by rolling up the legs of his slacks and putting a bathrobe on him. Of course he'll want to wear tennis shoes and boxing gloves. The dumber he can be in his role, the better!

In introducing the famous boxer, the sportscaster must use every possible superlative. When all of the accomplishments of the noted fighter have been shared, he enters and is interviewed in

[3]Shared by Joe Mason and Leon Mitchell, First Baptist Church, Sunday School Board, Nashville, Tennessee.

the following manner:

SPORTSCASTER:	Punchy, I hear that you just got out of the hospital. What was wrong?
PUNCHY:	Huh! Had operation!
SPORTSCASTER:	Was it serious?
PUNCHY:	No, just CANVAS removed from my back.
SPORTSCASTER:	How many fights have you had?
PUNCHY:	116.
SPORTSCASTER:	How many have you won?
PUNCHY:	All except the first 115. I'm currently on a winning streak.
SPORTSCASTER:	Tell us about your last fight.
PUNCHY:	My last fight was with Slim Magirk over in England.
SPORTSCASTER:	By the way, Punchy, I heard you had trouble crossing the Atlantic.
PUNCHY:	Yes, mainly because we were in the Pacific.
SPORTSCASTER:	What did you do before you became a boxer?
PUNCHY:	I was a lion hunter.
SPORTSCASTER:	Oh, how did you hunt lions?
PUNCHY:	Well, I hunted with a club.
SPORTSCASTER:	Well, isn't it a little dangerous to hunt that way?
PUNCHY:	No, it wasn't too bad. There were fifty of us in this club, and we would go out once a week.
SPORTSCASTER:	I've always wanted to ask a lion hunter something that has been bothering me. If you carry a torch through the jungle, is it true that the lions won't bother you?
PUNCHY:	Well, it depends on how fast you carry the torch.
SPORTSCASTER:	Punchy, where's your next fight?
PUNCHY:	Outdoor bout, Toronto, February 25th.
SPORTSCASTER:	Outdoor bout, Toronto, February 25th... It'll be a little cold, won't it?
PUNCHY:	Well, yeah, but then we'll have our gloves on.
SPORTSCASTER:	Have you ever fought any big name fighters?

PUNCHY:	Cassius Clay.
SPORTSCASTER:	How did you come out?
PUNCHY:	I had him scared to death in the second round.
SPORTSCASTER:	Scared to death? Cassius Clay?
PUNCHY:	Yeah! He thought he'd killed me!
SPORTSCASTER:	Well, there is one last thing I would like to ask you, Punchy. I noticed you have been thumbing your nose. I've always wondered why a boxer thumbs his nose. Can you tell us?
PUNCHY:	Oh, you mean this *(thumbs his nose a couple times)*? I don't know why those other guys do it, but me, I've got a cold.
SPORTSCASTER:	Oh, I see. Well, thanks a lot for the interview, Punchy. Let's give him a big hand. *(Punchy exits.)*

From Nine to Five

Rebecca Tune Young

Scene: An office, equipped with two desks, a filing cabinet, big clock on the wall, suggestion box, telephone, typewriter, coatrack, large baskets of envelopes, box of chocolates, and stacks of papers.

Characters: Hysteria, Deleria, Mr. Wump (who wears a sign saying, "I am the boss"), and Mrs. McMop.

(Mr. Wump is seated at his desk. Hysteria comes in. Mr. Wump points to clock.)

HYSTERIA:	Why shouldn't that old clock always be on time? It just stays here! *(As she hangs up coat, she passes suggestion box.)* By the way, Mr. Wump, the suggestion box is full.

Mr. Wump:	Fine! Call the janitor and have him burn it. And, may I ask, where is Deleria?
Hysteria:	I'm sure Deleria is working this morning, Mr. Wump. Her desk is here.
Deleria	*(comes rushing in):* I know you didn't buzz for me now, Mr. Wump. I'm answering for your buzz from yesterday.
Mr. Wump:	Deleria, where is that contract from the Snutzlote Company?
Deleria:	Just a minute, Mr. Wump, I'll find it. *(Begins tearing through the files beginning with A. Finally in desperation)* I've looked for that contract under everything from A to Z, Mr. Wump. Can you suggest any other letters? *(Gets blindfold from drawer and puts it on.)*
Mr. Wump:	Deleria, what are you doing?
Deleria:	Oh, it's perfectly all right, Mr. Wump. I find things much quicker this way. *(Goes right to it, hands it to Mr. Wump, and begins straightening files after removing blindfold.)* I could really speed up my filing if I had more wastebaskets.
Hysteria	*(carrying basket of mail):* Goodness, are we swamped with mail this morning, Mr. Wump! All these came back for postage. Guess I'd better call the post office. *(Begins to dial number.)* Hello, is this the post office? This is the Wump Company. Have you any sticky envelopes? We've got a bunch of stamps at the office that have lost their glue. You don't? Oh, well . . . thanks, anyway. *(Hangs up and turns to Deleria.)* Speaking of post offices, Deleria, did you see that picture of the man who's wanted in seventeen states. How can any one man be so popular?
Deleria:	Goodness, Hysteria, look at that clock. Do you see what time it is? Let's go. *(Leaves office and*

FUN WITH PREPARED SKITS/CHAPTER 3

	goes to table off stage. Coffee cups on table. Third worker joins them from the office.)
NEW WORKER:	I'm new around here. Can you girls tell me when we have a work break?
HYSTERIA:	Sure, we work all the time.
DELERIA:	And we're broke all the time. This watch my boyfriend gave me for Christmas is just what I need ... something I can pawn.
HYSTERIA:	Well, so long. We'll see you 'round. Guess we'd better get back to the salt mines. *(As they enter the office, Mr. Wump wakes up from nap and begins appearing to be busy.)*
DELERIA:	The boss comes in early, leaves late, and works like a beaver. What's he trying to do—impress us?
MR. WUMP:	Hysteria, get me that order from the "We Need It Company."
DELERIA	*(picks up paper from desk):* This is the third time they've cancelled this order. If you don't hurry and rush it out, they won't want it.
MR. WUMP:	Deleria, I will not have you giving me orders. I am the boss!
DELERIA:	My goodness, Mr. Wump, it's lunch time. Can't you finish screaming at us when we get back?
HYSTERIA:	As long as you're going to take a nap, Mr. Wump, how about making decisions on some of these things you wanted to "sleep on." *(Gives him stacks and piles of papers. Both walk out and hang "Out to Lunch" sign on door.)*
DELERIA:	I should have heeded the horoscope today. It just was not a good day for me to come to work.
HYSTERIA:	Before we go back I'd like to get my liniment prescription refilled. My back is o.k. now, but it's the only perfume my boyfriend has ever noticed. *(Seat themselves at table.)*

DELERIA: Speaking of medicine, I think I'd better get a checkup soon. It's getting where in the mornings, I can't fall back to sleep after I shut off the alarm. *(They order and waitress brings back huge plates of food piled high.)*

HYSTERIA: You know, Deleria, Calorie gave me this new diet that skips a meal a day. For breakfast I eat lunch, right now I eat dinner, and for dinner I eat tomorrow's breakfast.

DELERIA: Staying off peanut butter has sure helped me. But I still keep plenty of it. Since nobody at our house eats it, it's a real economy.

HYSTERIA: Guess we'd better get on our way. I've got to try to figure out some of those fancy words he's using now. We should never have given him that dictionary for Christmas!

DELERIA: And to think we paid so much for it, and he gave us the worst cologne he's given us in five years!

HYSTERIA: And the very idea of making us eat marshmallows instead of peanutbrittle just because he's declared antinoise week. *(Enters office and removes sign.)*

DELERIA: I'd like to borrow your new *Saturday Evening Post* until Mr. Wump comes back.

HYSTERIA: *(Phone rings.)* The Wump Company. Well, how should I know you had the wrong number? You don't sound any more confused than our usual calls. *(Hangs up. Then dials number to call a friend.)* Hello, is this you, Coma? Just thought I'd call you to tell you that _____ got her engagement ring back. I know she's not going to marry Didget, but it's the same ring. Now she's engaged to the fellow who was sent out by the finance company to repossess it. Oops, guess I'd better hang up. Here comes Mr. Wump.

MR. WUMP: Hysteria, this dinky little error of yours has cost my company $2,000.

HYSTERIA: Well, at least, it makes a girl feel she's getting somewhere!

MR. WUMP: Here, take these letters. *(Just as she seats herself next to his desk the phone rings. She answers from his desk while he impatiently strums the desk with his fingernails.)*

HYSTERIA: The Wump Company. Oh, hello, Nostalgia. Well, first you take a cup of flour, four eggs, mix with a cup of syrup, and cook for a half hour. Shall I hold the phone while you try it?

MR. WUMP *(rises from chair, slaps desk, and yells):* Hysteria, you're fired!

DELERIA: Hysteria, I declare to you that I just couldn't stay on this diet without these chocolates to tide me over.

HYSTERIA: Well, I'm glad somebody can enjoy them. I guess I won't be able to afford any more. He just fired me again. Well, it does give me a perfect excuse for staying home tomorrow. I'll just look for a temporary job until my charm course starts to work. *(Both put on coats and leave office. Phone rings.)*

MRS. MCMOP: Well, I'm not exactly his secretary, but if it's confidential I'll be glad to take the message!

The Night Before Christmas

Beverly Hammack

This clever dramatization was originally written for college students but has been done by all ages, junior high and above.

FUN WITH PREPARED SKITS/CHAPTER 3

Be sure to have at least two good rehearsals with all props so that backstage work can be perfectly timed with the narrative. Use an all-male or all-female cast.

Characters

Narrator
Ma
Pa
Sound-effects crew
Santa
The Jerk

Stage Setting

Bed *(a pallet will do)*
Window *(made of paper or cloth curtains)*
Fireplace, upstage center *(This can be made from Dennison crepe paper and cardboard.)*

If a stage is not available, the skit can be just as successfully done without a special setting. The imagination can easily supply the window, fireplace, and bed.

Narrator stands to one side out of the line of action or reads from a microphone, unseen.

'Twas the night before Christmas
And all through the house
Not a creature was stirring—they didn't have any spoons—
Not even a mouse—he didn't have one either—
The stockings were hung *(carries out stockings and hangs them, also hangs up a sign reading C-A-R-E)*
By the chimney with care,
In hopes that St. Nicholas soon would be there.
The children were snestled all bug in their neds
    were nestled all snug in their beds
While visions of sugarplums did their physical

FUN WITH PREPARED SKITS/CHAPTER 3

    exercises in their heads.
And Ma in her kerchief and I in my cap *(two girls dressed as*
    MA *and* PA *come out and get in bed)*
Had just settled our brains—and we use that loosely—
For a long winter's nap.
When out on the lawn there arose such a clatter *(dead silence)*
(Loudly) When out on the lawn there arose such a clatter
    (more silence)
(Louder) When out on the lawn there arose such a clatter!
Come on, clatter, arise! *(bedlam breaks loose backstage)*
I sprang from my bed (PA *gets up, stretches, yawns, and moseys*
    over to the window)
To see what was the matter.
Away to the window I flew like a flash *(moves over slowly)*
Tore open the shutter *(tears up paper shutter)* and threw up the
    sash *(take off sash and throw it high in the air).*
The moon on the breast of the new fallen snow *(have a crash*
    backstage when "fallen" is read)
Gave a luster of midday to objects below,
When what to my wandering eyes should appear
But a miniature sleigh—this is a killer—and eight tiny sparkle-
    darlings, reindeer, that is.
With a little old driver so lively and quick—could it be a jet?—
    could it be a bird?— could it be Superman?—
I knew in a moment it must be St. Nick.
More rapid than eagles his coursers they came.
And he whistled and shouted and called them "by name"
    (backstage persons shout out, "By name, by name, by name")
Now, Dasher, now Dancer, now Prancer and Vicks, On Comet,
    on Cupid, on Donder, on Blitzkrieg, Old Dutch, and
    Ajax *(person from backstage sticks head out and says,*
    "What do they have to do with this?" to which reader
    answers, "We're just trying to make a cleaning.")
To the top of the porch, to the top of the wall

Now dash away, dash away, dash away, dash away, dash away
    (someone yells from backstage "Broken record")
Dash away all.
As dry leaves that before the wild hurricane fly *(on these two
    lines read the punctuation "comma," "period," etc.)*
When they meet with an obstacle, mount to the sky—
I'm not supposed to read those—
So up to the housetop the coursers they flew
With a sleigh full of toys and St. Nicholas, too.
And then in a twinkling I heard on the roof
The prancing and pawing of each little hoof *(every-
    one backstage stomps)*
As I drew in my head and was turning around
Down the chimney St. Nicholas came with a bound.
    (Santa crawls through hole in fireplace)
He was dressed all in fur from his head to his foot
And his clothes were all tarnished with ashes and soot.
A bundle of toys he had flung on his back
And he looked like a peddler—Fuller Brush man—just
    opening his pack.
His eyes how they twinkled, his dimples: How? Merry?
His cheeks were like roses
His nose like a cherry
His droll little mouth was drawn like a bow
And the beard on his chin was as white as the snow—
    Burma Shave! Burma Shave! A beard that's rough and
    overgrown is better than a chaperon! Burma Shave!
    Burma Shave!
The stump of a pipe—oh, I can't read that here—
And the smoke—oh, no, not that either—
He had a bored—I mean a broad face and a little
    round belly
That shook when he laughed like a bowl full of jelly.
He was chubby and plump (SANTA *should be a very tall lean
    person with no stomach whatsoever)*

A right jolly old elf
And I laughed when I saw him in spite of myself (PA *laughs*)
A wink of his eye—the flirt—and a hist of his twead,
    I mean a twist of his head
Soon gave me to know I had nothing to dread.
He spoke not a word—the main reason women can't be Santa
    Claus—
But went straight to his work,
And filled all the stockings; and turned with a jerk
    (*person marked* JERK *comes out and* SANTA *picks him up
    and turns around with him*)
And laying his finger aside of his nose
And giving a nod, up the chimney he rose
He sprang to his sleigh, to his team gave a whistle—
Now wonder why he didn't put that whistle in my stocking—
I could have used it better than the team—
And away they all flew like the down of a thistle
But I heard him exclaim ere he drove out of sight
(*all backstage yell together*)
"Merry Christmas to all, and to all a good night!"

The Witches and the Crows
Helen F. McKee

Characters

Farmer John
Bill, his son
Charnoff
Hannah
King Crow

Joe and George Crow
Hepzibah Crow
Other crows if desired

Setting

A wooded area on Farmer John's land. This can be achieved by painted scenery or simply by using signs to indicate the setting.

Costumes

Charnoff and Hannah should be dressed as witches. The crows can wear black leotards with black sweaters, or merely wear signs telling that they are crows.

Properties

Two brooms, one large black kettle, and a magic wand (stick wrapped with foil). Small sticks to be gathered by Charnoff.

Scene 1

(*As the scene opens,* FARMER JOHN *and his son* BILL *are putting the finishing touches to a Halloween witch they have made in the woods to frighten crows.* CHARNOFF *is a happy witch and should not be made to look ugly.*)

BILL:	She surely looks like a witch. This is the best scarecrow we ever made. Wait until the boys see our two witches. It will really put them in the mood for Halloween.
FARMER JOHN:	All I want this witch to do is to get rid of the crows. I can't imagine where they came from. But they do say crows will travel as far as 200 miles to find a new hunting and feeding place.
BILL:	I guess they found it all right. Half our corn is gone.

FARMER JOHN:	If they keep stealing it, there won't be any left in another week *(puts pointed hat on witch)*.
BILL:	She almost looks real. Here *(putting broom beside her)*, we almost forgot this.
FARMER JOHN:	Your mother will wonder what we've been doing all this time. *(They go toward left exit.)*
BILL:	Let's call her Charnoff. Doesn't she look spooky, with the moon and all? Goodby, Charnoff, give the crows a good scare. *(Exit left.)*
CHARNOFF	*(stretches, straightens her dress, and looks up at trees as* HANNAH, *another witch, enters left on broomstick)*: How round the moon is, just perfect for Halloween.
HANNAH	*(going toward* CHARNOFF*)*: Good evening, Sister. Are we alone?
CHARNOFF	*(laughing)*: Ha, ha, ha, ha. I know the crows are watching us. Do be careful what you say.
HANNAH	*(in a loud whisper)*: What are you going to do about them?
CHARNOFF:	Make soup. *(In a loud, cackling voice)* Come now, Sister, you know how fond I am of crow soup.
HANNAH:	Not me. I'm tired of crow soup. I like sparrow soup better.
CHARNOFF:	We can have both. I'll make soup from half the crows *(waves her magic wand in the air)*. With this, I can turn the other half into sparrows, and then you can make sparrow soup. Get the kettle,

	Hannah, while I find wood for the fire. (HANNAH *exits left and brings in a large iron kettle while* CHARNOFF *picks up twigs for a fire. This action takes place near left exit. In the meantime,* KING CROW *tiptoes to right stage followed by* JOE, GEORGE, *and* HEPZIBAH CROW.)
KING CROW:	Dddddddid yyyyyyou see wwwwwwhat I saw?
JOE AND GEORGE CROW	*(together):* Our enemies, the witches.
HEPZIBAH CROW:	We can't stay here. They'll make soup of us.
KING CROW:	Or turn us into sparrows. . . . What a terrible fate. You're right, Hepzibah, we must go at once. *(Whispering)* Caw, caw, caw. *(The crows come from the forest and huddle in a circle around* KING CROW, *who whispers to them, and then tiptoes off right followed by the rest.)*
CHARNOFF	*(takes* HANNAH's *hand and they dance around a large black kettle chanting in cracked voices):* Fiddledeedee, Fiddledeedee, Soup for you, And soup for me, No more crows, No, siree, We'll trick them with Our witchery. *(As they stop dancing,* HANNAH *calls like a crow.)*
HANNAH:	Caw, caw, caw, caw. *(The two witches look all around them.)* Caw, caw, caw.

CHARNOFF: They've gone, thank goodness.
HANNAH: You don't think they're trying to trick us? You know, Sister, there's nothing foxier than a crow.
CHARNOFF: I know, Hannah, but they've gone. Come, the moon is full. Did you bring your broomstick? We mustn't disappoint the children. I know one little boy who has been waiting ever so long for this Halloween so he could see a witch riding a broomstick.
HANNAH: Could we visit Oscar Owl and Jenny Goblin?
CHARNOFF: If we hurry. We've done our good deed for today. Tomorrow will soon be here, so come, Sister. *(She picks up her broomstick and glides off left, followed by* HANNAH.*)*

The Story of Gransel and Hettal

Nancy James Sayers

Characters

Narrator, who is not seen
Gransel, a scrawny, dried-up boy
Hettal, a girl played by a huge boy
Father, a very dramatic, bedraggled person
Mother, a real knockout, complete with false eyelashes
Witch, same person as Mother, only the costume changes

Scene 1

(A small shack in the woods; trees and flowers are growing in the yard.)

NARRATOR: Once upon a time, a long time ago, there lived a man who had two lovely children: Gransel and Hettal. Gransel was a strong, healthy boy who loved to play in the woods and sing in answer to all the calls of nature about him. *(Enter a scrawny, dried-up boy who stumbles over his feet as he skips onto the stage. He yodels off-key.)*

This man also had a lovely daughter, Hettal, who was his heart's delight. She had a voice which sounded like the nightingale that sang around the cottage. *(Enter a huge boy dressed as a girl, complete with a yarn wig. "She" dances clumsily around and sings in an off-key bass voice.)*

But in spite of these two bright spots in his life, he was unhappy. His wife had died, and he had remarried—a silly old hag who didn't love his dear children. *(Enter the "dizzy blond" type of girl, chewing gum and filing her nails. She stops at mid stage and speaks to the children, who are huddled together.)*

MOTHER: Dah-lings! *(The children act as if they are frightened to death, and so the mother turns to the audience and speaks.)* Nyeah! *(Gestures with hand and exits; the children begin to play together, relieved that she has gone.)*

GRANSEL: Oh, Hettal, let's pretend that we have food to eat. Here, let this be the table. *(The table is only a figment of their imagination.)*

HETTAL: Oh, what a goody-goody idea. Here, have a moon pie.

GRANSEL: That's yummy, yummy to my empty tummy. *(Enter FATHER, who is worn-looking and worried. He very*

FUN WITH PREPARED SKITS/CHAPTER 3

dramatically clasps his hands together, wrings them, and then puts them to his head. He staggers around a bit and then speaks.)

FATHER: Oh, my beautiful children, the witch—I mean your mother—wants you to take a walk . . . you know, into the woods to search for strawberries. *(To himself):* Alas, alack, I know what she has in mind. . . .

GRANSEL: Oh, goody, goody—strawberries!

HETTAL: They'll be delicious with our regular meal of water.

GRANSEL: Let's go, Hettal! *(They go off the stage into the woods;* MOTHER *enters.)*

MOTHER: Oh, at last . . . *(gazing into the woods).* Now tell me, where's the money, honey?

FATHER *(still dramatically):* Alas, alack, there is no money. And now I have no children, either. Did *you* think *I* had *money?*

MOTHER: Look, Bud, you'd better have. It took my simple . . . my mind a long time to think of a way to ditch those brats. Now, where's the dough, Joe?

FATHER: Alas, alack, there is no dough, either . . . not even for bread! Woe is me . . . my lovely babies . . . gone forever. They will never find their way out of yon dark forest.

MOTHER: I'm going to find *my* way out if you don't come up with the cash, Dash.

FATHER: Alas, alack, you don't even know my name . . . and to think you married me for my money.

MOTHER: Just give me a couple of grand, Dan.

FATHER *(completely out of character for this line):* You're getting warm! *(He is referring to the name, Dan.)*

MOTHER: You're lazy and good-for-nothing, and to top it all, you're broke. I'm leaving you. I just happen to have my suitcase packed.

FATHER: Alas, alack, you never unpacked it. *(The* MOTHER *retrieves her suitcase from the house and huffily*

	goes off into the woods.)
NARRATOR:	The poor father is now completely grief-stricken and falls upon the ground in deep sorrow. *(The FATHER falls and has a childlike tantrum, kicking up his feet and waving his hands.)*
NARRATOR:	After some time, he regains control of himself and arises with new determination.
FATHER:	Hark! All is not lost. I shall go into yon forest and *seek* my children. They may even have the strawberries by now. *(The FATHER exits; the curtain is drawn.)*

Scene 2

(A candy house with lollipop trees, suckers, etc. Beside the house is a large box marked OVEN.*)*

NARRATOR:	Deep in the forest, far from their home, little do GRANSEL and HETTAL realize that they are about to discover something more wonderful than the delicious strawberries they set out to find. But look, what is this? Oh, no! A witch! *(The WITCH has appeared in the doorway of the house. She is obviously the same person as the mother in Scene 1. She is dressed as a witch. Her vacuum cleaner is parked in front of the house.)*
WITCH:	Ha-ha-ha, ho-ho-ho, I'll get those kids and I'll get his dough! Wheeee! But hark, they are coming. *(The WITCH slips back into the house and GRANSEL and HETTAL appear from the woods.)*
HETTAL:	Gransel, Gransel, look!
GRANSEL	*(disgustedly):* Hettal, you know Father told us to look for strawberries. . . . I ask you now, does that look like strawberries to you?
HETTAL:	It looks like food to me, and I'm hungry. Yeowwww! (HETTAL *tears into the house and eats everything*

	in sight. GRANSEL *thinks for a moment, and then joins* HETTAL; *then the* WITCH *enters.)*
WITCH:	Nibble, nibble like a mousie, who's that nibbling at my housie?
GRANSEL:	Who're you kidding? You can see she eats like a horse!
HETTAL:	Say, Witch, you look familiar.
WITCH:	Don't get wise . . . in the story you're supposed to eat, not talk.
HETTAL:	That's what I had in mind. Let's go, Gransel. *(They both eat heartily.)*
FATHER	*(voice comes from offstage):* Alas, alack, my poor little children. I'll never find them.
HETTAL	*(mumbling because her mouth is full):* Father, Father, come and see!
GRANSEL:	Look, Father, . . . food! *(The* WITCH *appears at the door and the* FATHER *enters from the woods.)*
FATHER:	Whoopee! *(The* FATHER *joins the children in eating the goodies. Then he spies the* WITCH *in the doorway.)*
FATHER:	Wow! *(at* WITCH)
WITCH:	Where's the dough, Joe?
FATHER:	Oops, I thought I recognized you. Into the oven, kids. *(They all grab the witch and throw her into the oven.)*
GRANSEL	*(eyeing the oven):* Oh, goody, goody, *gingerbread!*
HETTAL:	Father, you came just in time.
FATHER:	I thought sure I'd read you this story before . . . but now we can eat all we want. Have a lollipop, Gransel.
CHILDREN:	Oh, goody, goody, good.
NARRATOR:	And they all got fat and lived on "Metrecal" forever! *(As the curtain closes, they are all stuffing themselves on candy.)*

CHAPTER FOUR

MELODRAMA

Abigail Stands Fast

Mike Stuart

This script is funniest when done by an all-male cast. Choose five men or boys who are well liked by everybody and success is already assured.

Characters

Mother, a poor widow
Abigail, the daughter
The Villain
The Hero
The Announcer

Stage Setting

2 chairs
a piece of cloth, needle, and thread
funny book or magazine for Abigail

ANNOUNCER: Ladies and gentlemen, this evening we are happy to present an *A-1, high-class, top-notch*, dramatic drammer, entitled "Abigail Stands Fast." First, however, let me present the great and glorious cast of this A-1, high-class, top-notch dramatic drammer.

Playing the part of the sweet, little ole mother is _____ (Whistler's Mother) _____. (MOTHER *enters, takes a pose, and freezes.*)

Playing the part of the beautiful and charming heroine of our dramatic drammer is _____ (Miss America) _____. (ABIGAIL *enters and freezes.*)

Portraying the part of the sinister and evil Villain is _____ (Pound of Flesh) _____. (VILLAIN *enters and strikes a pose and freezes.*)

Last, but far from the lesser of the evils, I present _____ (Cassius Clay) _____, portraying the chivalrous hero. (HERO *enters and takes pose.*)

And now—we turn back the clock fifty years or so to the humble living room of the McGraw farmhouse. Oh, by the way, I am sure you will want to "boo" and "hiss" the Villain, and our Hero and Heroine will appreciate your cheers. So, if you ladies will kindly remove your hats—and if you gents will refrain from chewing tobacco, we'll get on with the play. And now—under the sponsorship of Sneed's Sweet Snuff, we present the A-1, high-class, top-notch dramatic drammer, "Abigail Stands Fast." (VILLAIN *and* HERO *exit.* ABIGAIL *and* MOTHER *sit.* ABIGAIL *reads a funny book and chews gum.* MOTHER *sews.*)

Act I

(*After about thirty seconds, there is a knock at the door.* MOTHER *and* ABIGAIL *look at each other as if they had not heard the* VILLAIN *at the door a dozen or more times.* MOTHER *gets up and hobbles to the door and opens it. The* VILLAIN *springs into the room.*)

Mother	*(wailing)*: Oh, no, not you!
Villain	*(sinister):* Yes, *it is I!*
Mother:	Oh, no, not you!
Villain:	Yes, it is I.
Mother:	Oh, no, not you!
Villain:	Yes, it is I, and I have come for the mortgage!
Mother:	Oh, no, not the mortgage.
Villain:	Yes, the mortgage.
Mother:	Oh, no, not the mortgage.
Villain:	Yes, the mortgage.
Mother:	Oh, no, not the mortgage.
Villain:	Yes, the mortgage or your daughter's hand in marriage!
Abigail:	We have no money to pay off the mortgage.
Mother:	You can't take my *darling, precious, lovable, adorable* Abigail!
Villain:	Either the mortgage or Abigail in marriage!
Abigail:	Please give us more time to get the money!
Villain:	No! Either pay or ... marry!
Mother	*(pleadingly)*: Give us until tomorrow, Mr. Villain!

(Villain *walks back and forth trying to make a decision.* Abigail *and* Mother *clutch each other's arms in fear.* Villain *suddenly turns to them and they almost fall backward.*)

Villain:	Until tomorrow it is! But when I return, have the mortgage or else! *(He exits.* Mother *and* Abigail *freeze.)*
Announcer:	Will the Villain return? Will Abigail be able to get the money? Will Mother finish her sewing? Will help come? Will Abigail stand fast? Act II in one moment.
	But now a word from our sponsor, Sneed's Sweet Snuff—the snuff that makes your lip so *round,* so *firm,* so fully packed. When you have the urge to sniff snuff, sniff Sneed's Sweet Snuff!

And now a letter from one of our satisfied customers!

DEAR FRIENDS:

My name is _____. I am only _____ years old, but I must admit that I felt much older before I started dipping Sneed's. I woke up every morning with headaches and that tired run-down feeling. But my main trouble centered in my wooden leg. I found that it was slowly but surely rotting away! Oh happy day when _____ told me about Sneed's and what it had done for her life! Since I started dipping *Sneed's* I no longer have headaches and that tired, run-down feeling. Thanks to Sneed's, new life has come into me. No longer do I fear the rotting of my wooden leg! In fact, I now have to carry a hatchet around—to keep the sprouts chopped off!

I know what you mean when you say, "A treat instead of a treatment."
                      Signed: _____

Thank you, thank you! Miss _____. We are mailing you twenty-five cartons of Sneed's.

And now for Act II of "Abigail Stands Fast." You will remember the dilemma which Abigail and her dear little ole mother are in! Will the Villain return? Will Abigail be able to get the money? Will Mother finish her sewing? Will help come? Will Abigail stand fast? Act II!

Act II

(MOTHER *and* ABIGAIL *unfreeze and repeat the business they engaged in during Act I. There is a loud knock at the door as in*

Act I. MOTHER *opens door,* VILLAIN *springs in.)*

MOTHER: Oh, no, not you!
VILLAIN: Yes, it is I!
MOTHER: Oh, no, not you!
VILLAIN: Yes, it is I!
MOTHER: Oh, no, not you!
VILLAIN: Yes, it is I, and I have come for the mortgage.
MOTHER: Oh, no, not the mortgage!
VILLAIN: Yes, the mortgage.
MOTHER: Oh, no, not the mortgage!
VILLAIN: Yes, the mortgage.
MOTHER: Oh, no, not the mortgage!
VILLAIN: Yes, the mortgage or your daughter's hand in marriage.
ABIGAIL: But we still don't have the money, honey!
VILLAIN: Then you must be my wife!
MOTHER *(grabs* ABIGAIL's *hand):* You can't take my *darling, precious, lovable, adorable* Abigail!
VILLAIN *(grabs Abigail's other hand):* Yes, I must have Abigail's hand since you cannot produce the money.

(They pull ABIGAIL *in rhythm, accenting the pull with each word, "Yes," "No," "Yes," "No." They say the words and pull her about five times. They freeze as knocking is heard at the door.)*

ANNOUNCER: Who is at the door? Friend or foe? Will the Villain win? Will Mother finish her sewing? Will Abigail stand fast? Act III in one moment.

And now a word from our sponsor, "Sneed's Sweet Snuff." _____ of _____ _____ Church, _____ says, and we quote, "I predict that by ____, every pastor in _____ will have turned to Sneed's—even as our church staff and our deacons have done! Are you having trouble getting folks to come to Training Union? Just lay in a stock of Sneed's—the dip that fits the lip!"

Thank you, _____, for that encouraging word. Fifty cartons of Sneed's will be speeded your way with our compliments!

And now—back to the A-1, high-class, top-notch, dramatic drammer, "Abigail Stands Fast." You will remember the situation which is: Who is at the door? Friend, or foe? Will the Villain win? Will Mother finish her sewing? Will Abigail stand fast? Act III!

Act III

(Knocking continues as the three characters unfreeze. ABIGAIL breaks from VILLAIN and runs into audience.)

ABIGAIL: Help! Help! Save me! Somebody save me. Help! Help! Help! *(ABIGAIL hops on the lap of some football player or other person everybody knows and likes.)*

HERO *(enters room triumphantly):* Never fear! The Hero has arrived. I am here to save you, my dear Abigail, and your sweet mother from this wretched VILLAIN!

ABIGAIL *(running to HERO):* Oh, my Hero! *(ABIGAIL picks HERO up and swings him around a couple times.)*

MOTHER: Oh, we will be saved!

VILLAIN: Leave, Hero! No one invited you to this wedding party! Can't you see I'm about to leave with my wife?

ABIGAIL: But I don't want to be your wife!

HERO: *(HERO goes over to VILLAIN and takes out a frilly, silk handkerchief from his pocket and shoos the VILLAIN out. The VILLAIN is as frightened as if the handkerchief were a sword or gun.)* O.K. Out with you, you wretched Villain. Leave forever and forever this *darling, precious, lovable, adorable*

Abigail and her dear mother alone. (*A terrible fight takes place offstage.* MOTHER *and* ABIGAIL *clutch each other's arms in fear. The* VILLAIN *comes in, sneering at the audience.*)

VILLAIN: Hee, hee, hee! These things don't always end "happily ever after." Come, Abigail! (VILLAIN *pulls her from the stage as the* MOTHER *follows crying.*)

MOTHER: Oh, my *poor, darling, precious, lovable, adorable* Abigail!

"A Mellerdrammer"

Agnes Pylant

Characters: Ma, Pa, Nellie, Elmer, and Smithers
Time: A bitter-cold night
Scene: The shabby living room of Ma and Pa. Ma, Pa, and Nellie are hovering over the scant fire on the hearth.

PA: It is a bitter-cold night. No living critter should be out!

MA: But we'uns will be out this time tomorrow night if a miracle don't happen.

PA: That Smithers is a demon! If he would give us a little time we could pay off the mortgage.

MA: But he won't.

NELLIE (*very dramatically*): I could save our home if I only would. (*She weeps.*)

PA: You mean by marrying that scoundrel? I had rather see ye dead!

MA: No, Nellie. I'm a-countin' on a miracle to save us. (*A knock is heard at the door.*)

Maybe that is the miracle now. Nellie, open the door. (NELLIE *opens the door and* SMITHERS, *the typical villain, enters. He laughs a diabolical laugh and attempts to seize* NELLIE *in his arms.*)

SMITHERS: Ah-ha! Well, well, well! (*Laughs.*) I thought a night like this would make it easier for my darling to decide to marry me. It is mighty bad not to have a roof over your head when the north wind howls and the ground is icy. What do you say, my proud beauty?

NELLIE: No! A thousand times no!

MA: Two thousand times no!

PA (*in a voice of thunder*): A million times no!

SMITHERS (*angrily*): All right, if that is the way you want it! You will come crawling to me yet, O haughty princess, and then it will be too late! (*He backs toward the door as he speaks. The door opens slowly. Two hands reach in and grasp* SMITHERS *by the throat. It is* ELMER, *the hero. He is very small of stature, but what a man!*)

ELMER: You swine! You scum! I ought to choke you to death and I aim to a little later. But right now this will do!

(*He sits in a chair and turns* SMITHERS *over his knees.* NELLIE *takes off her slipper and hands it to* ELMER *who proceeds to paddle* SMITHERS *with all his might. The poor villain cries and screams and kicks.*)

ELMER: Will you be good?

SMITHERS: Yes, sir!

ELMER: Will you let my girl alone?

SMITHERS: Yes, sir!

ELMER (*stands him on his feet, takes out his wallet, and dramatically hands over the mortgage money to* SMITHERS): There is your dough! Now, get out! (*He draws back his foot and directs a hard kick toward* SMITHERS *who steps swiftly aside.* ELMER *sits hard upon the floor.* SMITHERS *leaves hurriedly, muttering,* "Foiled again!" ELMER *sits on the floor and howls and rubs himself.* NELLIE, PA, *and* MA *kneel about him offering him handkerchiefs and exclaiming over him,* "My hero!" *and* "My miracle!")

Blown with the Breeze

James Keith McNair

Characters

Scarlet O'Carpenter .... Heroine
(antebellum gown with hoopskirt, long curls; carries fan or frilly parasol)
Charlotte .... Scarlet's Cousin
(hoopskirt, hair over one shoulder; carries small purse containing gun)
Beauregard Bowman .... Villain
(black suit, black string bow tie, black top hat, black cape; carries black cane and dueling pistols in pocket; wears black mustache)
Percival Pettus .... Hero
(white suit, pink shirt, red and white striped vest, large pink bow tie, flat straw hat, white shoes, red cane)
Junior .... Scarlet's Baby
(largest man available; long white baby gown with ruffles, ruffled bonnet with large bow under chin; carries huge bottle)
Baby .... ?
(pink gown, large pink bow in hair; carries stuffed animal)

Suggested Background Music

Songs of Stephen Foster and other songs suggestive of the South

(Curtain opens to reveal SCARLET *rocking on veranda of her plantation mansion; songs of Stephen Foster are heard in background, played in an old-fashioned piano style.)*

NARRATOR: Long, long ago in an era of magnolias and moonlight, antebellum mansions and hoopskirts, there lived a beautiful young widow named Scarlet O'Carpenter. Her life had been gay and carefree as she enjoyed plantation life prior to the Civil War. But suddenly she found herself in quite a predicament. Her dashing young husband had fallen into the Mississippi River and drowned, leaving her and her young child alone in the world to see after the plantation. Money became scarce to the point that she was on the verge of losing the family home which she loved so dearly. There was a way to save her plantation, but it was a horrible thought to young Scarlet! However, her cousin Charlotte had come to live with her and sought to provide encouragement and help. *(Enter* CHARLOTTE.*)*

SCARLET: Oh, Charlotte, I'm so distraught and troubled. I simply do not know where to turn or what to do. I hate so much to lose my plantation home, but there seems to be no choice.

CHARLOTTE: Well, you know you could marry that riverboat gambler, Beauregard Bowman. Why, he's just flipped over you.

SCARLET: Hush, hush, sweet Charlotte! I'd rather lose everything I have than to marry that worthless, villainous scum of the earth Beauregard Bowman! And besides, you know that my heart has been promised to that dashing, young, and perfectly

	adorable Percival Pettus.
CHARLOTTE:	But he's so poor. You can't marry him. We'd all starve to death.
SCARLET:	He may be poor, but he's so gorgeous, sweet, kind, considerate, manly, handsome, dashing—
CHARLOTTE:	Well, speaking of Percival, here he comes now.
PERCIVAL	(*entering from left*): Scarlet! (*Sigh*)
CHARLOTTE	(*disgusted*): Well, I'll leave you two alone and go see about Junior.
PERCIVAL:	Scarlet, my darling, marry me today and we'll be so happy forever and ever. (*Kneels and sings "I Love You Truly."*)
SCARLET:	But Percival, you know that I'm broke and so are you. We'd starve. And I'd lose my beloved old plantation to Beauregard Bowman. Although I love you, it looks as if I will be forced to marry that scoundrel Bowman.
PERCIVAL:	No! I'll save you somehow. Just have faith in me. (SCARLET *and* PERCIVAL *embrace as* CHARLOTTE *enters.*)
CHARLOTTE:	Percival Pettus, I'll teach you to kiss my cousin!
SCARLET:	Oh, Charlotte, that won't be necessary. He already knows how!
PERCIVAL:	I must be going, and try to figure out how to save you. (*Exit* PERCIVAL.)
CHARLOTTE:	Surely you can't consider marrying that poverty-stricken cotton picker. (JUNIOR *is heard crying offstage.*)
SCARLET:	Oh, my darling little baby wants his mother. Come on out here, my precious. (JUNIOR *crawls out, sits in* SCARLET's *lap as she sings "Baby Face" and feeds him his bottle.*)
CHARLOTTE:	Scarlet, here comes Beauregard Bowman with the usual smirk on his face.
SCARLET:	Oh, my, what does he want now? (*Enter* BEAURE-

	GARD *from right.*)
BEAUREGARD:	Good evening, my Scarlet, Miss Charlotte, and darling little Junior. (*Pats* JUNIOR, *who bites his hand; aside to audience: "The little monster!"*)
SCARLET:	Charlotte, take Junior into the house away from this madman. (*Exit* CHARLOTTE *and* JUNIOR.)
BEAUREGARD:	Scarlet, I can't put it off any longer. Your beauty has haunted me day and night. I'm miserable when I'm away from the fragrance of your loveliness and enchantment. Say you'll marry me and I'll save your plantation, and we can live in delight forever.
SCARLET	(*sings*): No, no, a thousand times no! You cannot buy my caresses. No, no, a thousand times no! I'd rather die than say yes!
BEAUREGARD:	Then I have no choice but to foreclose your mortgage and your home will become mine, all mine, and you and Junior will be out in the cold by Christmas Eve. (*Change time to fit occasion of presentation.*)
SCARLET:	Oh, what must I do? (*Enter Percival.*)
PERCIVAL:	Never fear, your hero is here. (*Slaps* BEAUREGARD *with his glove and challenges him to a duel.*) Sir, I challenge you. The winner will own this plantation and the hand of Scarlet.
BEAUREGARD:	I accept your challenge. Let's get on with it. (*Select pistols, pace off, turn and shoot.* BEAUREGARD *is hit, dies in grand style.* CHARLOTTE *has entered during the counting off.*)
BEAUREGARD	(*dying*): This just kills me!
SCARLET:	Oh, Percival, my hero, my love! (SCARLET *starts to run to* PERCIVAL; CHARLOTTE *pulls gun and shoots* SCARLET, *who dies in grand style.*)
CHARLOTTE:	Now, my darling Percival, you are all mine, and this house is ours, just as we planned!

PERCIVAL: Charlotte, my darling! (CHARLOTTE *and* PERCIVAL *embrace; enter* JUNIOR, *who picks up gun dropped by* CHARLOTTE *and shoots them both; they die in each other's arms.* JUNIOR *crawls up into rocking chair and begins to take bottle.*)

NARRATOR: And so the tragic story of "Blown with the Breeze" has come to an end, but as usual someone lives happily ever after! (BABY GIRL *enters and the two babies embrace.*)

Curtain

The Featherweight Champ
or
Tickled to Death

Jan Nisbet Boyd

Cast: Hero—Dangerous Dan
Heroine—Devastating Dixie
Villain—Evil Ellery
Heroine's Grandfather—Sincere Sam

NARRATOR: Devastating Dixie is pacing up and down the small ranch house on the 2-Way-Squeeze Ranch. Anxiously she looks at her watch. Nervously she chews her fingernails. Back and forth she paces. Suddenly Sincere Sam enters. She turns quickly and says—

DIXIE: Sincere!

NARRATOR: He turns away and does not answer. She catches his sleeve and cries—

DIXIE:	Did you bring the money?
NARRATOR:	He replies—
SINCERE:	Uh-uh.
NARRATOR:	She cries—
DIXIE:	But, Grandfather! Evil Ellery is coming today and the rent is due!
SINCERE:	Ah couldn't help it, gal. Some rustler stole all mah cattle before ah could sell 'em. I ain't got no money!
NARRATOR:	She turns away in despair.
DIXIE:	What shall we do?
SINCERE:	You could marry Evil Ellery. He likes blonds.
DIXIE:	Never! *(She picks up bottle with "dye" written on it in large letters.)* I'll die first!
NARRATOR:	They continue to pace about the room. Both are covered with gloom. (NARRATOR *sifts artificial snow over both from large can marked GLOOM.*) Time passes. (NARRATOR *walks across stage with a sign saying TIME.*) Suddenly a knock is heard and Evil Ellery sweeps in. *(He has a long cape thrown over his arm. Makes dramatic entrance, then starts brushing off his cape with a small clothes brush.)*
DIXIE:	Evil Ellery!
ELLERY:	I have come for the rent!
DIXIE:	Please give us more time!
ELLERY:	I want the money!
DIXIE:	Give us more time!
ELLERY:	The money!
DIXIE:	More time!
ELLERY:	If you got the money, honey, I got the time!
DIXIE:	Oh, please have mercy!
ELLERY:	I'd rather have the money!
NARRATOR:	At this crucial moment, the door is again flung open and Dangerous Dan enters.

DIXIE:	Dangerous!
DANGEROUS:	Dixie!
DIXIE:	Dangerous!
DANGEROUS:	Dixie!
DIXIE:	Dangerous!
NARRATOR:	Dangerous draws himself up, straightens his tie, and strides purposefully across the room to Dixie. *(He grabs her hand and starts shaking it.)*
DANGEROUS:	Mighty glad to see yah, gal!
NARRATOR:	Suddenly Dangerous becomes aware that Evil Ellery is trying to sneak out the door. He draws a feather and challenges him. Evil Ellery tries to escape, but Dangerous has his number. *(Pulls out number.)* After three stabs of the feather, Evil Ellery falls to the floor—tickled to death.
DIXIE:	Oh, Dangerous! You were so brave!
DANGEROUS:	Was I, Dixie?
DIXIE:	Oh, yes, Dangerous!
DANGEROUS:	Aw, Dixie!
NARRATOR:	And so, a hero receives a hero's reward.
SINCERE	*(striding across the room and shaking* DANGEROUS' *hand):* Ah'm mighty proud of you, my boy!

The Rhyme's the Crime
or
The Verse Is Yet to Come

Frank Hart Smith

This piece is a pantomime, a melodrama in rhyme. All stage directions, costuming, and so forth, can be determined from the text. The reader reads very melodramatically. The players exaggerate every action. They mouth the words as the reader reads them. You may want to have boys playing all the parts. Two or three good rehearsals will be necessary to make the presentation go smoothly.

Characters

>Reader
>Unhappy Pappy
>Unruly Julie
>Unstable Mable
>Unshaven Craven
>Untidy Friday
>Unafraid Wade

READER:
>This is a story o'erflowing with drammer—
>Undying like Shakespeare, a real superwhammer!
>No dally, no dilly, it's time to commence
>Hereto and forthwith our players come hence:
>Here's UNHAPPY PAPPY—the dad in this play,
>And then his two daughters,
>>who've turned his hair gray;
>
>First: UNRULY JULIE—who is cute but not sweet;
>Then: UNSTABLE MABLE—who writes with her feet.
>Now: UNSHAVEN CRAVEN—on whom MABLE dotes
>(he only can translate her footwritten notes).
>And: UNTIDY FRIDAY—whom JULIE doth seek
>(he's not around often, just one day a week).
>Last to appear in our great cavalcade
>Is the violent, vile villain—it's UNAFRAID WADE!
>
>The scene: a plantation in nineteen ought ten;
>UNHAPPY PAPPY has gone broke again.
>He strides back and forth, clasps his head in his hands,

And listens appalled as the villain demands,
"I, UNAFRAID WADE, do promise forthwith
That at midnight, no later, on August the fifth,
If you, UNHAPPY PAPPY, have not paid your rent,
Then I'll marry your daughter." That was all. Then he went.

Poor UNHAPPY PAPPY, alone and perplexed,
Pulls at his hair and appears sorely vexed.
UNHAPPY PAPPY, what most his heart grieves:
"What will I do with the daughter he leaves?"
Then, in a flash, he sees both his gals,
First JULIE, then MABLE—and with them, their pals.
UNRULY JULIE is playing croquet
With UNTIDY FRIDAY, who gets in her way.
"I'll show you! I'll knock you from here to Yazoo!
Were this ball your head, you'd know how I love you!"
"Farewell," he then murmurs, "this you'll never see—
Your work done by Friday." Exit he, then she.

So JULIE is gone and PAPPY'S eyes meet
His UNSTABLE MABLE, who writes with her feet.
To UNSHAVEN CRAVEN she's writing a line,
"Will you, bearded wonder, be my valentine?"
Translating the note in fervor and pain,
UNSHAVEN CRAVEN replies, "All is vain!
I love you, adore you, you make my heart beat,
But I'd never get used to your dirty old feet!"

Then MABLE is gone and Craven is too,
and UNHAPPY PAPPY is still in a stew.
It's August the fifth and midnight is near,
And UNAFRAID WADE comes forth with a leer:
"I've come for the money or else for my bride!"
UNHAPPY PAPPY is queasy inside.
He calls for his JULIE and MABLE, the dears.

He tells them the problem, he lays bare his fears.
UNRULY JULIE is first to react—
UNAFRAID WADE is tackled, attacked.
"He's mighty cute, and I claim him. He's mine!"
UNSTABLE MABLE takes her time, pens a line,
"If one must marry to save the old place,
I'll sacrifice, *I'll* bear the disgrace!"

UNAFRAID WADE—bruised, beaten, battered,
Actually finds himself fluently flattered.
JULIE is chosen by him to be wed,
And UNHAPPY PAPPY is happy instead.
And UNSTABLE MABLE, who lost without glammer,
Is twiddling her toes writing this kind of drammer.

There's some sort of moral here to be found.
It's not on the surface, it's deep and profound.
It could be that tackles unruly are neat,
It could be the value of writing with feet,
It could be that Pappy shouldn't be in a stew,
It could be that villains always get their just due,
Whatever it is, it's way underground.
That's what we said—it's deep and profound!

CHAPTER FIVE

MUSICAL SKITS

Othello[1]

Wilma Mintier

When adequately prepared, this mock opera is one of the best and is appropriate for use with any age group, junior high and above. Some of the old tunes will be unfamiliar to young people, so plenty of rehearsal time will need to be scheduled. If possible, start working three or four weeks in advance so that tunes and lyrics can be learned perfectly. Only then can the players completely throw themselves into the parts.

Lead the cast to sing in exaggerated opera style. Be careful not to overdo the thing. This spoils the fun!

Work for clarity of words. This is the one point at which most groups fail in presenting mock opera. Each word must be carefully enunciated with special care given to the elongation of vowel sounds. From the very beginning, work at being understood. Call in a few people who do not know the script and let them listen to a rehearsal. Put a bell in each person's hands and ask him to ring it each time a word can't be understood.

---

[1] Helen and Larry Eisenberg, *The Pleasure Chest* (Nashville: The Parthenon Press, 1949), p. 109. Used by permission.

FUN WITH MUSICAL SKITS/CHAPTER 5

Characters

Othello
Desdemon
Iago
Emilia
Friendly Undertaker
Fire Dep't Crew
Chorus

Costumes

Shakespearean costumes (bathrobes, towels, and scarves) will add color. Some groups have created authentic costumes to add to the atmosphere of the script.

Stage Setting

This piece can be done with a bare stage, except for the final scene which requires a sofa and several pillows. The sofa can be made with three or four straight chairs covered with a blanket or sheet.

Prologue

(The chorus and principals enter and sing to the tune of "Long, Long Ago.")

ALL: Come now and look at our tragical show,
Of Othello and Desdemon.
This play will move even your hard heart of stone,
Poor Othello, poor Desdemon.
They loved each other clear to distraction,
He got so jealous he stopped her heart's action,
Then stabbed himself to his own satisfaction,
Poor Othello, poor Desdemon.

OTHELLO: I am the villain who lived long ago:
I'm Othello, I'm Othello.
My nasty temper caused my wife lots of woe,
I'm Othello, I'm Othello.

	I wish I'd never seen that handkerchief,
	It was the thing that caused us all the grief,
	I had to kill my poor self for relief,
	I'm Othello, I'm Othello.
DESDEMON:	I am the heroine who died in disgrace,
	I'm Desdemon! I'm Desdemon!
	Died with a sofa pillow stuffed in my face,
	I'm Desdemon! I'm Desdemon!
	Othello thought that I loved other men,
	Innocent was I, and quite free from that sin,
	I loved him truly in spite of his din,
	I'm Desdemon, I'm Desdemon.
IAGO:	I am Iago, the villain, you know,
	I'm Iago, I'm Iago.
	Blackguard am I who has caused all the woe,
	I'm Iago, I'm Iago.
	Oh, how I tortured that man and his wife,
	Until he snuffed out the poor lady's life,
	Turned on himself and inserted a knife,
	I'm Iago, I'm Iago.
EMILIA:	I am the lady-in-waiting, you see
	Emilia, Emilia.
	Iago can find it a cinch to use me.
	Emilia, Emilia.
	I found that kerchief that caused all the woe,
	I found the villain and made him glad to the toe,
	Little did I guess that my man was bad, tho,
	Emilia, Emilia.

(*All exit as pianist begins to play "Red River Valley."*)

Scene 1

(DESDEMON *enters, followed by* OTHELLO.)
OTHELLO *(to tune of "Red River Valley")*:

    Good-by, darling, I must leave you,
    Tho it breaks my heart to go,

> Something tells me I am needed,
> If we're going to fight the foe.
> Here's a token at the parting,
> And to you I'll e'er be true,
> See the ships are in the harbor,
> Good-by, darling, and adieu.

DESDEMON (*to tune of "Old Black Joe"*):
> I thank you for this handkerchief, my dear,
> 'Twill serve to wipe away my grief and tears,
> I'll cherish it with loving care, my dear,
> And never lose it, that I promise, have no fear!
> (*Exit Othello. Desdemon stands forsaken. Enter Emilia, who skips about the room as she sings.*)

EMILIA (*to tune of "Yankee Doodle"*):
> Othello has gone to sea, but do not feel so badly.
> It won't bring him back to thee to look so glum and sadly,
> Othello has gone away, Othello has gone away,
> Othello will fight, they say,
> Until they've conquered Turkey.
> (EMILIA *and* DESDEMON *exit.*)

Scene 2

(OTHELLO *enters singing, followed by* IAGO.)

OTHELLO (*to tune of "Spanish Cavalier"*):
> I'm home from the wars, from the wars I've returned.
> To greet my dear wife, Desdemona,
> And if I know wimmen, she's waiting, eyes brimming,
> Attired in her nicest silk kimona.

IAGO (*Tune—"My Bonnie Lies Over the Ocean"*):
> Othello, I'm glad you've come home, sir,
> It's time you came back to your wife,
> I'd hate for you longer to roam, sir,

Lest it should cause trouble and strife.
Take care, take care,
Lest it should cause trouble and strife, and strife,
Take care, take care, lest it should cause trouble
    and strife.

I saw her this morn at her window,
I saw the red rose in her hair,
I wonder for whom she was watching,
She looked so adorably fair.
Take care, take care, she looked so adorably fair,
    fair, fair,
Take care, take care, she looked so adorably fair.

I think that I saw her give Cassio
A smile as she stood on the stair,
I think that she gave to him also,
The rose that she took from her hair.
Take care, take care, the rose that she took from
    her hair, hair, hair!
Take care, take care, the rose that she took from
    her hair.
(*Exit* IAGO. *Enter* DESDEMON.)

DESDEMON (*to tune of "Maryland, My Maryland"*):

You find me waiting here for you; Othello, my
    Othello,
I've loyal been to you, and true; Othello, my
    Othello.
Since you've been gone, I've been so sad,
This handkerchief was all I had,
To cheer me up when I felt sad; Othello, my
    Othello.

OTHELLO (*to tune of "My Bonnie Lies Over the Ocean"*):

My head it is likely to bust, dear,
My head it is likely to break;

> If ladies weren't present, I'd cuss, dear,
> I have such a horrible ache.

DESDEMON *(to tune of the chorus of "My Bonnie Lies Over the Ocean"):*

> There, there, there, there,
> We'll wrap it up tight in this handkerchief,
> There, there, there, there,
> Then maybe it won't cause you such grief.

OTHELLO *(speaks):* Take it away! *(Drops handkerchief).*

(Exit DESDEMON and OTHELLO. Enter EMILIA who finds handkerchief.)

EMILIA *(to tune of "Juanita"):*

> Down on the floor here, a nice handkerchief I see,
> Sure, 'tis the same one, that he begged of me.
> How oft old Iago bade me steal it when I could,
> But I still refused him, I was quite too good.
> Found it, yes, I've found it,
> Finding's keeping, so they say,
> Found it, yes I've found it,
> He'll have it today!

(Enter IAGO. EMILIA gives him the handkerchief.)

IAGO *(to tune of "I've Benn Workin' on the Railroad"):*

> I've been hunting for this handkerchief,
> All the live long day.
> I've been wishing I could find it,
> Just to prove the things I say.
> Now I'll make Othello jealous,
> Cause him grief and pain,
> Now, I guess that I'll have fixed him,
> When he meets his wife again. *(Exit, followed by Emilia.)*

Scene 3

(DESDEMON *enters, followed by* OTHELLO.)

OTHELLO (*Tune—"O Where, O Where Has My Little Dog Gone?"*):
O where, O where has my bandanna gone,
O where have you kept it hid?

DESDEMON: It's safely stored, and will treasured be,
You know I'm not one to kid.

OTHELLO: I believe, I think that you lie to me,
I think you gave it away.

DESDEMON: Oh, why do you hurt me and cause me such woe?
I couldn't; that's all I can say.

(*Exit* DESDEMON. OTHELLO *paces back and forth. Enter* IAGO.)

IAGO (*to tune of "Did You Ever See a Lassie?"*):
I have found the handkerchief, handkerchief, handkerchief,
I have found the handkerchief that she gave away.
She tossed it, she waved it, to Cassio she gave it,
Oh, I've found the handkerchief that she gave away. (*Exit.*)

OTHELLO (*to tune of "How Dry I Am"*):
How mad I am, how mad I am,
Nobody knows how mad I am. (*Exit.*)

(DESDEMON *enters and goes to the couch.*)

DESDEMON (*to tune of "Old Black Joe"*):
Gone are the days when my heart was young and gay,
Gone are my joys, they have fled so faraway,
Sadly I sigh for the days of long ago,
I hear his angry footsteps coming, O-THEL-LO!
He's coming, he's coming, and my head is bending low,

FUN WITH MUSICAL SKITS/CHAPTER 5

      I hear his angry footsteps coming, O-THEL-LO!
(Falls asleep on couch. Enter OTHELLO.*)*
OTHELLO *(to tune of "Clementine"):*
    O my darling, O my darling,
    O my darling Desdemon,
    You'll be lost and gone forever,
    Dreadful sorry, Desdemon.
    Fair thou wert, and like a fairy,
    But you played me for a sucker,
    You have played upon my heart strings,
    Now, I'll make you a harp plucker! *(Smothers her with cushion. Enter* EMILIA.*)*
EMILIA *(to tune of "Juanita," beginning with chorus):*
    'Thello, O, Othello, What in the world have you done?
    'Thello, O, Othello, she's an innocent one!
    Over that there kerchief,
    What an awful fuss you've made,
    You got hydrophobia,
    When 'twas just mislaid.
    Desdemon dropped it, once when you were cross and mad,
    Finding it I gave it, to my husband bad.
    Iago, Iago, used it then with wicked art.
    Iago. Iago *(HE LOOKS IN FROM WINGS WITH WICKED LEAR),*
    What a wretch thou art!
OTHELLO *(to tune of "Hot Time in the Old Town"):*
    I've killed you, I loved you best of all,
    In my grief, I'll stab myself and fall,
    When I'm gone, bring on the bearers-pall,
    There'll be some funerals in Venice tonight.
    (Stabs self.)
(Original ends here. One group added this epilogue for a "happy ending.")

Epilogue

FRIENDLY UNDERTAKER *(enters and sings to tune of "Old Gray Mare"):*
>This old play it ain't what it used to be,
>Ain't what it used to be, ain't what it used to be,
>This old play it ain't what it used to be,
>Many long years ago.

(Fire Dep't enters and revives the two.)
FRIENDLY UNDERTAKER *(to tune of "Yankee Doodle"):*
>For we called the fire department,
>Gave first aid to 'thello,
>On the maiden used pulmotor,
>And the grease of elbow.
>
>They were down, and now they're up,
>Toast of all the nation,
>Gratitude they give to arti-
>Ficial respiration!

Carmen[2]

NARRATOR: We welcome you to another performance of the grand old opera, *Carmen*, by the world famous _____ Opera Company. Now, as the lights dim, the conductor mounts the podium. *(Conductor strolls over to the piano and climbs up on it.)* We hear the strains of the magnificent overture. *(Pianist plays one note and a discord.)* As the curtain ascends *(someone stretched out on*

---

[2]From *Favorites from the Fun Festivals,* Jack Fellows and Recreation Staff, Ridgecrest Baptist Assembly, 1953. Used by permission.

FUN WITH MUSICAL SKITS/CHAPTER 5

the floor gets up and lifts a curtain), it is a hot and sticky day in Seville, Spain. CARMEN *and her fellow workers are standing in front of the Seville Glue Factory waiting for the mucilage machine to be fixed. We hear them as they sing:* (CARMEN *and three men workers sing the following words to the tune of Cornell's "Alma Mater."*)

> On our city's western border
> Stands the plant we love
> Mucilage and glue a-bubbling,
> We lift our smell above.

(Back to work whistle or siren)

NARRATOR: Just as the song ends, the back-to-work whistle blows and they all start to leave. Just before Carmen leaves, Don José, who is the third stirrup adjuster in the Spanish Cavalry, enters. Don José is madly in love with Carmen, but Carmen does not love José. All Carmen wants to do is get José's fine fast horse, Rocinante. Carmen needs Rocinante because the glue factory is running out of raw materials, and if she doesn't get Rocinante, the glue factory will go to pot. She rushes over to José and sings the hauntingly beautiful "Seguilda."

CARMEN *(sung to the tune of "Seguilda" from Carmen):*
Oh, Don José
Oh, don't you see
Rocinante is the horse for me? *(Repeat)*

DON JOSE: Oh, no, he ain't!
CARMEN: Oh, yes, he is!
DON JOSE: Oh, no, he ain't!
CARMEN: Oh, yes, he is!
NARRATOR: Just then Carmen realizes she must go, so she throws Don José a rose. *(The flower sticks to* CARMEN's *hand. She has to sling it off and then it sticks to the floor.)* This ends Act I. *(Curtain falls.)*

As the curtain raises for Act II, we see Carmen's true love, Escamillo, the toreador, shooting the bull with the board of directors of Toreadora Cuspidora, Spain's largest manufacturer of genuine cuspidors. We hear them as they sing the famous "Toreador Song."

ESCAMILLO AND THE THREE MEN: Toreadora, don't spit on the floor-a
Use the cuspidora,
That's what it's for-a.

NARRATOR: Just then Escamillo spies Carmen, who is Miss Mucilage Mixer and Postage Stamp Fixer of 1953, and rushes over to her. They sing....

ESCAMILLO: Do you love me?
CARMEN: Oh, yes, I love you!
ESCAMILLO: Then marry me!
CARMEN: But I can't marry you.
ESCAMILLO: Why can't you marry me?
CARMEN: I must marry Don José.
ESCAMILLO: But why must you marry Don José?
CARMEN (*speaks*): "A horse, a horse, my kingdom for a horse."
ESCAMILLO: I'm tired of this horsing around with you.
CARMEN: But all you ever do is shoot the bull. The bull? THE BULL!

NARRATOR: Carmen suddenly realizes a way out. She quickly talks Escamillo into giving her the bulls he kills to make glue. He readily agrees because his company, Toreadora Cuspidora, must have glue in the manufacture of their product. However, about this time a whiff of this unsavory affair reaches the nosey Senator McCartos and his Congressional Investigating Committee in the capitol. They quickly come to investigate. As they enter, they sing the great quartet. Quartet? *(Counts the*

FUN WITH MUSICAL SKITS/CHAPTER 5

quartet) Due to the change in the administration, El Presidente Iké thinks a trio will be more economical. They sing *(tune—"How Dry I Am")*

> One bull for one,
> Two bulls for two,
> Three bulls for three,
> And the glue factory for me.
> Oh, don't you see,
> The factory's been took
> And now poor Carmen
> Will get the book.

NARRATOR: After gathering all the information possible here, the committee retires to the glue factory to see what's in the wind there. Just then Don José enters. He sings passionately to Carmen.

DON JOSÉ: *(to tune of "String Along"):*
Stick around, stick around,
Stick around with me.

ESCAMILLO: Oh, no, that cannot be.

NARRATOR: Carmen, stuck between the two, is forced to make a decision. She does so in the famous aria, "Allegro Moderato Pizzicato Fortissimo."

CARMEN *(goes over to the conductor and sings):*
I wanta go home with you
Nobody else will do.

JOSÉ AND ESCAMILLO: No, no a thousand times no. (CARMEN *starts to leave with the conductor when* ESCAMILLO *and* DON JOSÉ *grab her arm. The conductor and narrator grab the other arm. They sing to the tune of the "Fight Song."*)
We're pulling hard for you, Carmen
C-A-R-M-E-N
In all kinds of weather
We'll all stick together
For C-A-R-M-E-N.

(Exeunt Omnes)

The Romance of Minnie Martin
or
"It Shouldn't Happen to a Dog"

Scene: Cabin in the hills

Characters:

    Minnie Martin—a poor little beautiful hill girl
    Grandmaw Martin—her poor old grandmaw
    Hiram Coy—Minnie's boyfriend
    Grandpaw Coy—Hiram's weak-eyed old grandpaw
    Sylvester "Joe" Sly—a cruel-hearted villain
    Lola Lane—who always gets what she wants
    Singing Group—an ensemble that sings the narration before and after each act

The singing group should be seated to the side of the stage and should stand each time they sing. They may use scripts but will need to rehearse together enough times to be able to stay together and make each word clearly understood.

Costuming and makeup can add much to this fun piece, so be sure to involve several people on committees to get costumes rounded up and beards and other makeup done.

Act I

Opening Song: Tune, "Ballad of Davy Crockett"

In a little cabin back in Arkansas, lived a little girlie with her old Grandmaw.
The gal's name was Minnie, and she was so sweet—she up and stole the heart of every man she chanced to meet.

(Chorus)

Minnie, Minnie Martin!
    Perty as she can be.
Minnie, Minnie Martin!
    Queen of the hill country.

Like every little girlie, Minnie loved a boy
But she was a Martin and Hiram was a Coy
Their families had been feudin' since 1892,
A feudin' and a fightin'—so what could Minnie do?

(Chorus)

Minnie's heart was broken and she cried all night,
She loved little Hiram till it really was a sight,
When he came courtin'—around the Martin place,
Minnie's dear old Grandmaw would shoot him in the face.

(Chorus)

(Scene opens with GRANDMAW *sitting in her rocker. She calls to* MINNIE *who is off stage.)*

GRANDMAW: Minnie child, come sit with me.
    Outside it is too dark
    You needn't think that Coy boy
    Will come tonight to spark.
    Come on my child, in here with me
    It's almost time for bed
    If Hiram comes around tonight,
    I'll shoot him in the head.

MINNIE *(as she enters)*: But Grandmaw, dear, I love him so
    He is the one for me.
    If I can't marry Hiram Coy
    I'll die of misery.

GRANDMAW: Then die, my little beauty proud,

	I'd rather see you dead
	Than know that you have gone astray
	and to a Coy have wed.
MINNIE:	But Grandmaw, dear, you are so cruel, and sometimes you are rude.
	You see, I do not understand what started all this feud.
GRANDMAW:	I do not know too much my child how this thing got its start.
	I only know the dirty Coys shot Grandpaw through the heart.
	Yer paw they shot in his left leg, yer brother in the neck.
	Yer maw, they shot her in the barn, and left her there, a *wreck!*
	Now let me warn you, Minnie gal, before I hit the hay.
	I'll kill those two remaining Coys, before my dying day.
	There's two of them, and two of us—we're women and they are men.
	But we'll show them that the weaker sex can be as tough as sin.
MINNIE:	Goodnight, goodnight, my Grandmaw, dear, I'll see you with the dawn.
	(*Aside*) Oh, Hiram, Hiram, please do come now that to bed she's gone.
	Take me in your arms, my dear, and say you love me true.
	Hiram love, I'm so alone, for one just ain't like two.
	(Chorus)
HIRAM	(*enters*): Minnie, Minnie, I've come at last, I'm sorry I'm so late.

FUN WITH MUSICAL SKITS/CHAPTER 5

	But Grandpaw has been watchin' me ever since we ate.
	He said he'd shoot me if I came to see you once again.
	He hates you Martin women because you killed our kin.
MINNIE:	Oh, Hiram love, you've come to me, you've chose the bitter way!
	Yer Grandpaw'll shoot you if you go, my Grandmaw if you stay.
	But Hiram, I'll remember you long after your cruel death!
	I'll ne'er forget your greasy face and your sweet onion breath.
HIRAM:	Nonsense, Minnie, do not talk so; this is not my last day!
	Can you not understand my sweet, I've come to take you away.
MINNIE:	Away? Away? To take me away? But who'll take care of stuff?
	Who'll tend the hogs and milk the cows, and go to town for snuff?
	Oh, no, my love, I cannot leave! Grandmaw might even cry.
	I think it would be better, love, if you would stay and die.
HIRAM:	Farewell, farewell, Minnie my sweet, I'll have to leave you too.
	Someday, perhaps, I'll come again. Till then will you be true?
MINNIE:	Oh, Hiram dear, you know my love for you will never end;
	I'll always be just yours alone! On that you can depend.

HIRAM: I love to hear you talk that way, I love to see you so . . .
Someday we will be married, but bye now, I must go. (*Exits*)

MINNIE: O life, thou are so cruel to me, I'm left alone to cry.
Hiram's gone to the city, and I think that I shall die.

(Chorus)

Act II

Opening Song:
In a little cabin back in Arkansas, lived a little girlie and her old Grandmaw. The gal's name was Minnie and she was so sad,
For she lost her lover who always made her glad.

(Chorus)

Two years had come and gone since Hiram went away,
Minnie was so lonesome till in the month of May
There came a city slicker to the hills of Arkansas
Minnie didn't know that he was runnin' from the law.

(Chorus)

The feller was a talker and he captured Minnie's heart;
He said he loved her truly and he really played it smart.
He spent his time a courtin' and diggin' in the soil;
He didn't tell poor Minnie that *he discovered oil.*

(Chorus)

(*Scene opens with* GRANDMAW *and* SLY *sitting and talking.*)

GRANDMAW:	Oh, Mr. Sly, I'm so glad you come back in these here hills,
	Ain't had so much excitement since we operated stills!
	Minnie is so happy that she's lighted up inside,
	Just think come Saturday my boy, she'll be your blushing bride.
SLY:	Oh, yes, Mrs. Martin, she'll be mine! Ah my, but ain't true love grand?
	And Saturday's our wedding day, at least that's what we planned.
	But I could wish it were today, I love my Minnie so,
	But let me call you "Grandmaw" now, and you just call me "Joe."
GRANDMAW:	Okay Joe, I'll call you that. Now help me find my dip,
	I declare I'm so excited the snuff done left my lip.
SLY:	Grandmaw, you're such a dear old girl, I'd do anything for you.
	I'm sorry that our wedding plans have got you in a stew.
	Minnie will be safe with me, she'll never know no harm.
	Now about a wedding present, perhaps the deed to the farm.
GRANDMAW:	I'm glad you'll treat my Minnie sweet, and supply her every need,
	But *my*, you *do* seem anxious, Joe, to get from me the deed.
SLY:	Of course I'll treat dear Minnie nice, and the deed, where is it, dear?
	I'll take care of it from now on, you need not have a fear.

GRANDMAW:	I'll go fetch it Joe, my son, but don't wait up for me.
	It's hid down by the river in a hollow chestnut tree. (*Leaves.*)
SLY:	Ha, ha, ha, ha! What she don't know is that she can't trust me.
	For when I get that deed, my friends, there'll be no sight of me.
	This place is worth a fortune cause there's oil under the land.
	Ha, ha! I just can't wait to get the money in my hand.
	What do I care about poor Minnie, and her old Grandmaw dear.
	I want the money and that's all, but hark, who's coming here?
MINNIE:	Oh, Joe my love, I cannot sleep, I had an awful dream!
	I dreamed that you were cruel to me; you even made me scream.
SLY:	Oh, Minnie Baby, don't you cry, don't worry, don't you fret!
	'Tis but a foolish nightmare caused by something that you et!
	I know the very thing you need to make you feel so gay
	Just take a little stroll with me; I'll drive your fears away. (MINNIE *and* SLY *exit.*)
GRANDMAW	(*comes rushing in*):
	Oh, Mr. Sly, I'm back, I'm back! Oh, dear, where can he be?
	This deed I want to give him, he'll keep it safe for me. (*Knock.*)
	Oh, my, there's someone at the door, and at this time of night!

FUN WITH MUSICAL SKITS/CHAPTER 5

	I'll run up and powder my face; I really look a fright.
LOLA	*(enters):* I've knocked and knocked and no one came, I'll come in anyway.
	What a terribly dirty house; but I've not long to stay.
	I'll find that dirty Sylvester Sly; he left me in the lurch,
	all dressed up in my weddin' gown and waitin' at the church.
	I knew when I fell in love with him, he's crooked as a barrel of snakes,
	Love struck me blind and left me dumb, and how my poor heart aches.
	He'll be sorry when I'm through with him; I'll shoot him with this gun.
	Six months I've traced Sylvester Sly, and now my searchin's done.
	I know he's livin' in this shack, courtin' his little honey.
	O, how I hate that evil man for stealin' all my money.
GRANDMAW	*(enters):* Well, hello, dear, and who are you? I'm sorry I'm so late.
	If there's one thing I hate to do, it's make a body wait.
LOLA:	Hello, old girl, my name is Lola; I'm huntin' for a friend.
	His name is Sly, *(aside)* and he is too, but he's coming to his end.
GRANDMAW:	Sly? Sly? You must mean Joe. He's going to be my son.
	He's marrying my little Minnie gal, the two they shall be one.

LOLA: What's that you say? A wedding day? Minnie and
my friend, Sly?
(*Aside*) Just wait until I get my hands upon that
dirty guy.
MINNIE (*enters*): Yes, I'm the Minnie of which you speak,
I'm pretty, too, I know.
And I'm in love with a gentleman whose best
friends call him "Joe."
But come, my dear, whoever you are; a battle's
'bout to begin
Between two Martin women and one of the Coy
men.
GRANDPAW COY (*enters and holds them up*):
Too late, too late, you foolish girls.
My, my, but ain't you cute?
With cheeks so red and eyes so blue,
you're almost too perty to shoot!
CHORUS: (*Fades in, singing "Minnie Martin."*)

Act III

Opening Song: In a little cabin back in Arkansas,
    things look tough for Minnie and her old
Grandmaw.
When Minnie was so happy,
    thinking 'bout her wedding day,
Grandpaw Coy prepares his gun
    to take her life away.

(Chorus)

GRANDPAW: As I was saying a minute ago, before being interrupted
I hate to shoot such lovely gals, with beauty
uncorrupted.

	I'll shoot you Martins one at a time; there'll be none left to grieve,
	Now are you ready for me to shoot? Women—prepare to leave!
SLY	*(enters and hits him on the head):* Minnie my love, I've saved your life. I hit him on the head.
	My but he hit the floor so hard, it's a wonder he ain't dead.
MINNIE:	Oh, Joe, you saved my life, I'll love you till I die.
	Now here's a friend I want you to meet, as sweet as cherry pie.
LOLA:	Thanks, Minnie, for the compliment, but "Joe" and I have met.
	His name was Sylvester then, I never shall forget,
	For he's a dirty crook you see, that I have come to kill. *(Reaches for gun in garter slightly below her knee.)*
	To see him dying in his blood will give my soul a thrill.
	I hate all dirty thievin' skunks; wear the shoe if it fits.
	Just remember, Sylvester Sly, whatever Lola wants, Lola gets.
SLY:	Oh, Lola love, why treat me so! Do you not understand?
	I'm marrying this gal for money, not love. There's oil in this here land.
	If you must shoot, then shoot the girl. We'll kill the old lady too.
	We'll sell this place for a million bucks, and half of it goes to you.
LOLA:	Oh, oh, what shall I do? Sylvester, I love you so.
	I'll do exactly as you said. Minnie gal, prepare to go!

GRANDMAW	*(enters and hits* LOLA*)*: Minnie gal, what's going on?
	What's this gal trying to do?
	Here, Joe, my son, is the deed to the farm.
	I'm glad to give it to you.
MINNIE:	Oh, Grandmaw dear, you've saved my life! I'll love you till I die.
	But you mustn't give the farm to Joe. He's not my kind of guy.
SLY	*(with* GRANDMAW's *gun)*: Too late, too late, Minnie, my gal.
	Ha, ha! I have the deed.
	I'll shoot you two and run away. I now have what I need.
MINNIE:	Oh, Joe, how can you be so cruel! You've deceived me all the time.
	What about Saturday's wedding? *(Aside)* I can't think of a word that will rhyme!
SLY:	Minnie gal, come Saturday, you'll be six feet under the ground.
	And as for old Sylvester Sly, he just won't be around.
	Ha, ha! Ho, ho! this is the end. Well—ain't you going to cry?
	The end of Minnie and her old Grandmaw; now girls, prepare to die.
HIRAM	*(enters and hits* SLY *on the head)*:
	Minnie, Minnie, I've come home; I will not let him kill.
	I'll turn him in to the constable, and he the jail will fill.
MINNIE:	Oh, Hiram, my love, you've saved my life; I'll love you till I die!
	And I have been *so true to you,* never *looked* at another guy.

HIRAM:	Don't lie to me, Minnie my love, but one thing I can see.
	You loved him then, you love me now, how important can it be?
MINNIE:	Hiram, Hiram, I've an idea. Will you marry me Saturday?
	Folks are coming for a wedding, and just what could I say?
GRANDPAW COY	*(coming to):* Of course, he'll marry you, little gal,
	Who are you by the way? Hiram my boy, where have you been?
	I just missed you yesterday. (GRANDMAW *picks up her gun and starts to shoot* GRANDPAW.)
MINNIE:	Oh, Grandmaw dear, put down your gun; it's time to end the feud!
	For Hiram and I will marry, and things will turn out good.
GRANDMAW:	What's that you say? We'll end the feud? Now Minnie we can't do that.
	Why what will all the neighbors say if you marry that little rat?
GRANDPAW:	What's that you say? You call my boy a rat? Just wait until I find my gun.
	I'll shoot you in the teeth old girl. Who said this feud was done? *(They exit.)*
MINNIE:	Hiram, my love, we're alone at last! Is there anything you'd like to say?
HIRAM:	Yes, you're a Martin, I'm a Coy. You'll be DEAD by SATURDAY! (MINNIE *runs screaming from the room with* HIRAM *after her. Or . . . if you have a spot, a complete blackout after the last line of Hiram's would be good.)*

Dr. Quack's Medicine Show

Cecil McGee, Steve Turner, and John Fullerton

This takeoff on the colorful old traveling medicine show has been successfully used with college students, junior highs, high schoolers, and adults. It can easily involve as many as forty or fifty people or can be done with a smaller cast.

Several full rehearsals will be needed to put the show together so that it will go smoothly. Much of the success of this piece depends upon Happy Jack and Dr. Quack, so these two characters should be carefully chosen.

Characters

Happy Jack
Dr. Quack
Mrs. Cornswable
Chorus
Extras

Opening Theme

(*The theme song, "Healthy Days Are Here Again," is played on the piano and any other instruments that are available. A fun band can be formed with combs (put a piece of tissue paper over the comb and hum through it), pots and pans from the kitchen, and toy band instruments. The* CHORUS *enters as the orchestra plays. They sing the theme song.* Tune: "Happy Days Are Here Again," published by Advanced Music Corporation, New York City, New York. Available in music stores, 75 cents.)

CHORUS: Healthy days are here again, again.
The skies are blue again, again.
Dr. Quack and Happy Jack are back.
Healthy days are here again.

FUN WITH MUSICAL SKITS/CHAPTER 5 121

HAPPY JACK *(with theme song played softly in background)*: Yes, friends, healthy days are here again, thanks to Dr. Quack and his world-renowned Medicine Show which has toured the great cities around the globe: Murfreesboro *(trumpet fanfare);* Goodlettsville *(trumpet fanfare);* and Paris, France *(trumpet fanfare).* And friends, here is the charming little lady whose club has made possible our appearance in your fair community. Ah, here is Mrs. Cornswable, wife of Mr. Cornswable, your beloved mayor.

MRS. CORNSWABLE *(wearing the most outlandish hat that can be created):* On behalf of the Dipsy Doodle Hat Club, of which I am president, welcome. In the absence of my husband, the mayor, may I present to you, Happy Jack, the key to our fair city *(dramatically unrolls and presents to* HAPPY JACK *an exaggerated cardboard key).*

HAPPY JACK *(kisses her hand):* On behalf of Dr. Quack and the personnel of our show, I would like to say that we are all touched deeply and, Madam, a special section has been reserved for your club in the second balcony. With this key you have unlocked the door of our hearts. And speaking of heart—friends, does yours have that "slight twitter" *(clock ticking into mike)* that causes you alarm? *(Alarm goes off in mike.)* We have good news for you, for right here—before your very eyes—is the towering spirit who will change your future (health?). We give you:

122 FUN WITH MUSICAL SKITS/CHAPTER 5

guar-an-teed or your mon-ey back. Do you ache? Is there pain? Do you think that you are go-ing in-sane? See Doc-tor Quack! See Doc-tor Quack! His rem-e-dies are guar-an-teed or your mon-ey back.

CHORUS *(speaking):* Your money back? Huh, just try to get it! *(The chorus exits as orchestra plays.)*

DR. QUACK *(with Eastern accent):* It is much delight to be here. I am sorry I not speak your language ... I

HAPPY JACK *(cutting in):* You understand, of course, that Dr.

Quack has been in our country only a few weeks and has not yet mastered our language. The revered doctor is acclaimed around the world for his medical accomplishments. Oh, Dame Fortune has smiled upon your fair city in sharing Dr. Quack and his magic trumpet! *(If a good trumpet player is not available, use whatever instrument you have.)* Let's give the doctor and his magic trumpet a big hand. (HAPPY JACK *leads the applause.)* Yes, friends, the doctor and his "magic trumpet" will thrill you with unbelievable things tonight. You will go away different because you came! Doubtless, there is something wrong with all of you, or you wouldn't be here! Doctor, the people wait!

DR. QUACK *(Goes out into audience. He stops and examines various people and gives humorous comments. To a good-natured large man that everyone likes, he says):* Sir, you are way out. I feex you. *(He toots on the horn. He then goes to a popular man and woman, looks them over carefully,* and says): As they say in your country, you are "all shot." *(He gives them a pill and toots his horn again. He then picks out a teen-age couple, looks them over knowingly, and says):* You two look seeck. I feex you! You have lovebird seeckness. *(As the doctor goes back to the stage, the pianist plays "Love Is a Many-Splendored Thing.")*

MAN: *(A man with a bumpy back comes forward out of the audience. The special effect is created by putting an inflated balloon under his shirt and coat.)*

HAPPY JACK: What can we do for you, young man?

MAN: I have a personality problem, and the girls don't like me!

DR. QUACK *(stepping up to examine him):* I feex you up!

HAPPY JACK *(leads man to table, gets him on table):* I assure you sir, all will be well.

DR. QUACK: *(Selects magic balm and hands it to* HAPPY JACK *who administers it and gives spiel about the power to penetrate.* DR. QUACK *is seated on a special, draped chair where he does his best concentration. Dry Ice in hot water under chair gives mystic effect.* DR. QUACK *rises and slowly moves his hand in front of his body, signifying that no more balm is needed. Toots horn.)*

HAPPY JACK *(bursts balloon, and in utter amazement says):* The little Doc has done it again—amazing! *(Turns man around to show audience that the bump is gone.)* It just happens that among our troupe we have a world-renowned singer who wrote a song that we would like to dedicate to our friend here. We give you _____, who will sing _____.

SOLOIST: *(sings something that is "pure corn.")*

DR. QUACK: What ees e'en de mell beg, Hoppy Jock?

HAPPY JACK: Ah, Doc, we have a huge box filled with thrilling letters from all over the world. *(Fishes in box for a mailbag and pulls out a small sack hardly large enough for more than one letter.)* Ah, yes, here is a letter from _____, such a charming little woman, and so devoted to the pursuit of health and medical knowledge. Yes, we say devoted, for when we played in her quaint little village, Buzzard Roost, she sat right there on the front row forty days and forty nights with her twelve children. (HAPPY JACK *reads her letter. A popular young man dressed as a woman from the mountains may be substituted to come forward and give a personal "testimony.")* Our thanks to Mrs. _____ for her word of cheer which has brightened our little corner of the world. And now our Quacky Jack Chorus comes to sing a special song in honor of Mrs. _____.

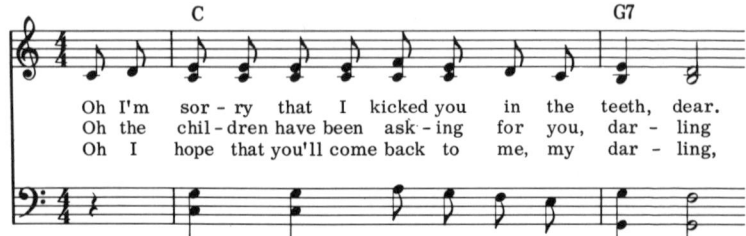

Oh I'm sor-ry that I kicked you in the teeth, dear.
Oh the chil-dren have been ask-ing for you, dar-ling
Oh I hope that you'll come back to me, my dar-ling,

FUN WITH MUSICAL SKITS/CHAPTER 5

125

And I'm on my bend-ed knee to you to-day. And I did it just be-cause that I love you, did-n't think that hit would make you go a-way. Go a-way, oh, go a-way. Did-n't think that hit would make you go a-

And their fac-es were so pit-i-ful to see, that I tuck-'em out and shot'em with the shot gun, just to putt-'em out of all their mis-e-ry. Mis-e-ry oh, mis-e-ry, just to putt-'em out of all their mis-e-

I'll try to make it up to you some-how. I'll ev-en help you do all the house work. And I'll get a mule to help you pull the plow. Pull the plow, oh, pull the plow, I will get a mule to help you pull the

FUN WITH MUSICAL SKITS/CHAPTER 5

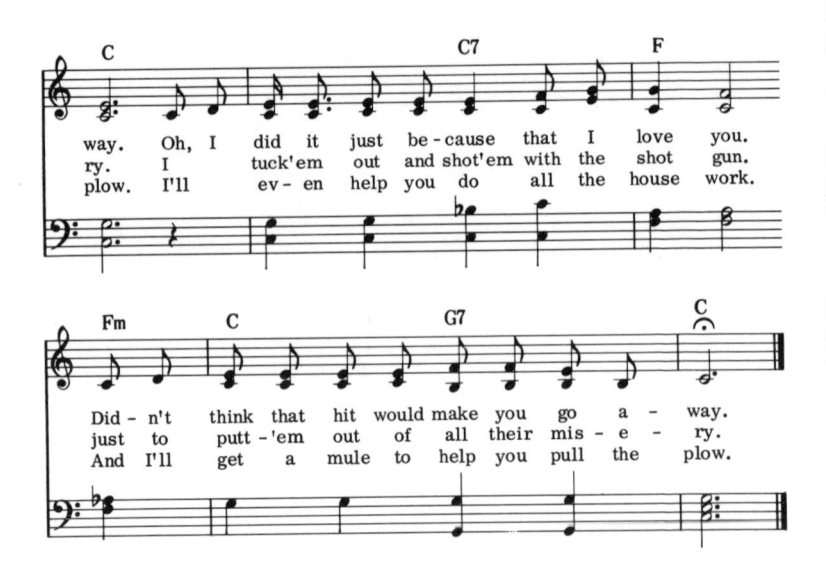

	way.	Oh, I	did it	just	be-cause	that I	love	you.
	ry.	I	tuck'em	out	and shot'em	with the	shot	gun.
	plow.	I'll	ev-en	help	you do	all the	house	work.

	Did-n't	think that	hit would make	you go	a-	way.
	just to	putt-'em out	of all their	mis-	e-	ry.
	And I'll	get a	mule to help	you pull	the	plow.

HAPPY JACK: Give 'em a hand, ladies and gentlemen! Ah, that great music really hits you hard! (*Introduces* CHORUS *members and says*): They are wanted all over the country because of their talent. Friends, when they came to our show they were helpless, hopeless, homeless, *monotones!* But our magic "melody mist" did the trick—absolute transformation! These chorus members have worked without pay simply to contribute to society! All they ask is their daily portion of "magic mist." Ladies and gentlemen, you too will cry for "magic mist." (*Two people from troupe go among audience with fly sprays, spraying some cheap, stinky perfume while chorus sings and plays instruments.* CHORUS *exits.*)

DR. QUACK: (*Gives "magic trumpet" message to* HAPPY JACK.)

HAPPY JACK: Oh, thank you, Doc. (*Speaks to audience.*) He has just reminded me of our most fabulous contribution to your welfare and happiness. This product will cure the itch and the backache; it will make the old young again. Ah, yes, you're dying to know what the little Doctor's latest discovery is—and we're going to do something we've never done before in the history of our show. We're going to give every person here a sample of this wonder product—"Can't Cure Candy." Included in each bag of candy there are fortunes *(each sack contains a humorous fortune)* and a few sacks contain a coupon entitling the holder to one of Dr. Quack's art masterpieces.

CHORUS: *(Goes among the audience giving out candy as* HAPPY JACK *describes some of the famous "originals" done by _____, the inimitable artist of Arabia. He reminds the people that the doctor has collected pieces from all over the world. A great deal of fun can be had collecting the humorous art pieces from somebody's attic or from the city dump.)*

HAPPY JACK: Any word, Doctor?

DR. QUACK: I rec-cog-neyes guh-rate art lovers in our midst. *(Throws kiss to audience.)*

OLD MAID: *(Boy dressed as old maid. Runs forward from audience "oohing" and "aahing".)* I never dreamed this thrilling thing would happen to me.

HAPPY JACK: Yes, Madam. Share the good news with us.

OLD MAID: Oh, my fortune! It says that I am going to meet a tall, dark, handsome stranger with white pearly teeth! *(Continues to show excitement.)*

DR. QUACK: *(Plays magic trumpet—*"Some Enchanted Evening"*)*

HAPPY JACK: *(Quotes first two lines of song to* OLD MAID *as trumpet music is played.)*

THE PHANTOM: *(Dressed in black with white or greenish makeup on face, enters. Two long, white, pearly tusks are sticking out of his mouth. The* OLD MAID *faints in his arms and is carried off by* PHANTOM.*)*

HAPPY JACK: Another customer made happy! Now all you people with coupons in your candy sack, come up and exchange them for an art masterpiece. *(As the people come,* HAPPY JACK *describes each piece as it is given to the proud owner!*

Next, Happy Jack *introduces a stunt. Any funny stunt that the group has not seen can be woven in here.)*
Woman: *(Leading big teen-ager dressed as a baby. She twitches neck and jaws as she comes forward pulling the brat along.)*
Happy Jack: And what's your trouble, young woman?
Woman: Ain't nuthin' wrong with me—hits my little dotter.
Happy Jack: And what's wrong with her?
Woman *(twitching as she speaks)*: She's—she's got "athletic feet."
Dr. Quack *(examines the girl and has an idea; toots horn.)*: I feex you! *(Uses big mop and dips it in a bucket and swabs the girl's feet; then gives child a beat-up teddy bear.* Woman *and child go away happy!)*
Happy Jack: And now we have a special feature to entertain you with: Suzena, the "wonder dog," of the North American Continent. And no less fabulous is his mistress, who is undoubtedly the most beautiful dog trainer in the world. Ladies and gentlemen, Lady Marlena and her wonder dog, Suzena. *(Comes on stage.)* You will be amazed, as I was, at the intelligence and grace of this little animal. Everyone please be just as quiet as possible so Suzena can concentrate and give her best performance.
Lady Marlena: First, Suzena would like to show you that she knows what I want her to do by a mere "position of the hand." (1. *Holds hand upward with thumb extended and dog sits on hind legs.* 2. *Holds palm of hand toward floor at waist level and dog lies on stomach.* 3. *Snaps finger and dog lies on back (optional).* 4. *Holds stick one foot from ground and dog jumps over it and lands on hind legs [pretends that she is unsteady by bouncing to front feet, then up].* 5. *Holds up a piece of candy and dog speaks for it by barking. [Trainer pretends she isn't speaking loudly enough and makes her speak second time.]* 6. *Extends hands and dog shakes hands.)* And now, Suzena would like to show you that she is a mathematician. *(Holds up fingers and dog barks for the number of fingers that are up.)* And now we come to Suzena's

favorite sport—jumping through a hoop. *(After two or three jumps, the dog interrupts the act with barking. The trainer pretends she is trying to give a message. She asks two or three times what it is she wants.)*

Suzena is trying to tell me that her powers of divulging intimate secrets are at work and there are some things she must reveal because it's overtaxing her mental capacities to keep them any longer. *(Dog barks.)* What? Oh, no! Oh, but you shouldn't reveal who has the dirtiest feet in the audience. It would be embarrassing. Well, all right. *(Dog goes to someone, comes back to stage, and barks again.)* What? Oh, no. Please, that would never do. Suzena tells me that someone in the audience has been secretly married for over a month. I really don't know what to do. She insists on revealing this secret. *(Dog starts toward audience.)* Oh, dear! *(Dog goes to that person in the audience.)* Suzena, please, let's go on to something else. This could get us in trouble. *(Dog leans up against trainer's leg.)*

And now we come to the most fabulous dog act that has ever been attempted. Suzena is the only dog in the world that even attempts it. She will walk the tight rope on her hind legs. *(Place chair at one end of rope for dog to hop up on; two people will hold the rope at the level of the chair; after several attempts to step onto the rope the helpers will lower the rope to the floor and the dog jumps down and walks across it. The dog then falls to her front feet a couple of times as she bows to the audience. She then stands sideways and wags her tail so the audience can see it.)* As her reward, I always give her some of Dr. Quack's potent tonic. She has her choice, of course. *(Dog chooses tonic. Trainer removes cap and places nipple on it and pretends to give it to the dog to drink. Dog skips around on stage as if full of energy, then bounces backstage. Trainer bows, then dog rushes back out and stands on hind legs and bows. To assure success in the dog act, choose two people for the dog and trainer who*

are favorites of the group. Then it will be delightful!)
HAPPY JACK: *(Introduces any other talent that may be needed to round out the show.)* Ah, as the time draws near for the close of our show tonight, dear friends, we give you once again our Quacky Jack Chorus to sing our theme song.
CHORUS: (Sings "Healthy Days Are Here Again.")

CHAPTER SIX

AUDIENCE PARTICIPATION SKITS

Nobility[1]

Ethel Bowers

Here is a stunt that can be used anywhere with any age group. Choose four outstanding people. Ask them to stand behind a long table, facing the audience. A knife and a fork are put on the table in front of each contestant. Each contestant begins with fifty points to his credit, but each time he makes a mistake he loses a point. Alert judges keep score. The leader reads the story and contestants must impersonate each character immediately and correctly. They cannot change a pose once assumed until the judges have counted the score. Characters and poses are:

CRUEL KING—Left hand on hip, right holds knife with blade up as a scepter; head high.

CRINGING QUEEN—Left hand over heart; right holds fork to plate, as in eating; head low.

PRETTY PRINCESS—Left hand in lap, drinks from glass or cup with right hand, little finger crooked gracefully; head tilted.

PROUD PRINCE—Arms folded on chest; head thrown back.

CAPTAIN OF THE GUARDS—Left hand at hip on imaginary scabbard; right hand as if drawing sword; head high, very arrogant.

---

[1] From *Parties, Plans, and Programs*, ed. Ethel Bowers (Washington, D.C.: National Recreation and Park Association). Used by permission.

If the leader drawls the C of "Cruel," "Cringing," and "Captain" and the Pr of "Pretty" and "Proud," he will add to the confusion and fun.

As the leader reads the story, those seated in the audience act out the following words:

"Thunder," "thundered," "yelled," "roared"—STAMP FEET
"Pounded"—SLAP KNEES OR TABLE
"Sound of breaking glass"—TAP GLASS LIGHTLY WITH SPOON (if used at a banquet)
"Clasping or wringing hands"
"Pulling hair"
"Gnashing teeth"
"Beating a tattoo with fingers"
"Pointing," etc.

Here is the story:

One dreadfully stormy evening, as the *thunder* rolled overhead, a CRUEL KING was seated at his banquet table. "Close the window," he *thundered* at the CAPTAIN OF THE GUARDS, "and get out of here!" Then the KING *pounded* on the table with his knife, "Why doesn't someone say something? Have you no tongues?" The CRINGING QUEEN clasped her hands and ventured to say, "My dear, should we not soon be seeking a Prince to be a husband to our Pretty Princess?" "No," *yelled* the KING, this time *pounding* the table with his fist. "She is but a child, and besides I'll have no Proud Prince disputing my decisions, nor a nincompoop around here either." The PRETTY PRINCESS *beat a nervous tattoo on the table with her fingers* and said softly, "Father dear, I met a man in the garden today—who, . . ."

"You met a man?" *roared* the KING, *pulling his hair* and *gnashing his teeth*. "I'll have any man found in my garden shot at sunrise by the CAPTAIN OF THE GUARDS."

Just then the *sound of breaking glass* was heard, and the CAPTAIN OF THE GUARD, greatly disheveled, threw open the door and dragged in the PROUD PRINCE. "Your Majesty the King," said the CAPTAIN OF THE GUARDS, "I found this man attempting to enter the castle by stealth."

"Shoot him at sunrise and ask his name afterwards," *roared* the CRUEL KING. Then spoke the CRINGING QUEEN, "This Proud Prince is my godchild, son of my dearest friend. Oh, King, you must not treat him so." The PROUD PRINCE turned to the PRINCESS and spoke endearingly, "Pretty Princess, from the moment I met you I loved you. I fear not to die. Give me the rose you wear in your hair, and I'll carry it to my grave."

"My Father the King," entreated the PRINCESS as she *wrung her hands* in despair, "this is the man whom I met today in the garden. I love him. You must not let my Prince die." Then spoke the QUEEN—now at last every inch a queen—"The Proud Prince shall marry our Princess and you, O King, shall not stop it!" With that the QUEEN threw pepper in the CRUEL KING's face, grabbed the hand of the PRINCESS, placed it in the hand of the PRINCE, knocked the CAPTAIN OF THE GUARDS on the head with an ox bone, pushed the PRINCE and PRINCESS out the door into the rain and the *thunder,* turned to the KING and *pointing* to an inner door, *roared,* "You go to bed!" The KING went!

The Trip to Mexico[2]

This impromptu skit involves a leader and three or four other persons. Choose persons that the audience likes very much if possible. Instruct all taking part that they must repeat what they hear in succession, then they must do what they see done and keep doing it until the end of the skit.

[2]This version was shared by Frank Hart Smith, Church Recreation Department, Baptist Sunday School Board, Nashville, Tennessee.

The leader begins by telling this to the person to his right:

"Last summer, I decided to take a trip to Mexico. When I got to the border, I asked the border policeman if I could go in. He said I would have to cut a lot of red tape first. So, I got out my scissors and cut the red tape."

The leader then begins to make a scissors-cutting motion with his right hand. He continues to do this throughout the skit. The one on the leader's right then proceeds to tell the person on his right what he has heard. He ends by cutting the red tape.

After the "cutting the red tape" has gone all the way down the line and all are "cutting," the leader tells the person on his right:

"I then asked the policeman if I could go in now, and he said 'Yes, you can go in now.'"

The leader nods his head affirmatively and keeps nodding it throughout the skit. He is now nodding his head and cutting at the same time. This portion goes all the way down the line.

Then the leader says to the one on his right, "The policeman was such a nice man to let me in Mexico that I waved good-by as we drove off." He then waves with his left hand and keeps waving. He is now waving, cutting, and nodding his head. The waving portion goes all the way down the line.

The leader then says to the one on his right: "When we got into Mexico City, we got a hotel. Well, the elevator in the hotel broke and started going up and down, up and down." Here the leader bends his knees and straightens up, bends and straightens up, keeping this up until the end. He is now bending, waving, cutting, and nodding.

After this has gone all the way down the line, the leader says: "On the elevator, this lady had a clock and it was broken, too. It kept going 'Cuckoo! Cuckoo! Cuckoo!'" He keeps saying, "Cuckoo!" until all are saying it. End the game with a round of applause for all taking part.

The King with the Terrible Temper[3]

(There are seven characters in this story. Divide those present into seven groups, each group taking the part of one of the characters. They say the sounds listed below every time their character is named in the story.)

Characters

1. The King with the Terrible Temper—"Grrrrrrrrrrrrrrrrr!"
2. The Short, Fat Daughter—"Kerplunk"
3. The Tall, Thin Daughter—long, prolonged whistle
4. The Very Beautiful Daughter—swoony sigh . . . "Ahhhhh"
5. The Handsome Young Prince—short and snappy: "Aha!"
6. His Trusty Steed—long whinny
7. Mergertroid, the Horrible Dragon—"Sizzle, sizzle, pip"

The Story

(Pause after each character named so group can sound off.)

Once upon a time, many years ago, there lived a KING with the Terrible Temper. Now this KING with the Terrible Temper was very proud of his three daughters—the SHORT, FAT DAUGHTER, the TALL, THIN DAUGHTER, and the VERY BEAUTIFUL DAUGHTER. But the KING with the Terrible Temper was very unhappy because into his kingdom had come MERGERTROID, the Horrible Dragon.

What made the KING with the Terrible Temper so unhappy was the fact that MERGERTROID, the Horrible Dragon had been slaying and eating inhabitants of the kingdom of the KING with the Terrible Temper. So—the KING with the Terrible Temper decreed that he would give in marriage any one of his three

---

[3]Used by permission of Lynn Rohrbough, *Handy Stunts* (30c), Cooperative Recreation Service, Inc., Box 333, Delaware, Ohio. Adaptation by Frank Hart Smith.

daughters—the SHORT, FAT DAUGHTER, the TALL, THIN DAUGHTER, or the VERY BEAUTIFUL DAUGHTER—to any knight who would slay MERGERTROID, the Horrible Dragon. . . . Day after day the knights came. But all of them were slain and eaten by MERGERTROID, the Horrible Dragon. This was very upsetting to the KING with the Terrible Temper, not to say what it was to the digestion of MERGERTROID, the Horrible Dragon.

But finally, into the kingdom of the KING with the Terrible Temper rode the HANDSOME YOUNG PRINCE on HIS TRUSTY STEED. Dismounting from HIS TRUSTY STEED, the HANDSOME YOUNG PRINCE said, "Oh, KING with the Terrible Temper, I have come to slay MERGERTROID, the Horrible Dragon." "Then go to it," cried the KING with the Terrible Temper. And to it the HANDSOME YOUNG PRINCE goed. Mounted upon HIS TRUSTY STEED, the HANDSOME YOUNG PRINCE went forth and he slew MERGERTROID, the Horrible Dragon. Cutting off the head of MERGERTROID, the Horrible Dragon, the HANDSOME YOUNG PRINCE, riding atop HIS TRUSTY STEED, went to the KING with the Terrible Temper.

Rejoicing, the KING with the Terrible Temper said, "Now, O HANDSOME YOUNG PRINCE, you may choose one of my daughters as your wife." The HANDSOME YOUNG PRINCE took one look at the SHORT, FAT DAUGHTER and turned green. The HANDSOME YOUNG PRINCE then took one look at the TALL, THIN DAUGHTER and turned purple. The HANDSOME YOUNG PRINCE then took one look at the VERY BEAUTIFUL DAUGHTER and he turned cartwheels! So—the HANDSOME YOUNG PRINCE and the VERY BEAUTIFUL DAUGHTER were married and they rode off on the TRUSTY STEED and they left the kingdom of the KING with the Terrible Temper and spent the rest of their lives hunting down and slaying descendants of MERGERTROID, the Horrible Dragon!

Starring You

Agnes Pylant

Says the LEADER: "A play has been arranged starring YOU. We have heard of your dramatic ability and are all eager to see you in a performance. So if you will be kind enough to act the story our narrator relates, we shall appreciate it so much. If you will do this for us, please tell us with a smile and by saying, 'I shall be delighted!'" (ALL *say in unison, "I shall be delighted."*)

The NARRATOR reads the "play," pausing for dramatic action and the speaking of lines. He indicates the time to speak and act with a movement of his hand. The capitalized words are those to be acted out or repeated.

NARRATOR: The scene is a little cabin high on a mountain side. A storm is raging. The heroine stands looking out through the single window. There IS A LOOK OF FEAR ON HER FACE. There is a crash of thunder and a flash of lightning. THE GIRL SCREAMS. SHE WRINGS HER HANDS. SHE SOBS. In a hoarse whisper she says, "O, MY DARLING, WHY DON'T YOU HURRY TO ME?" She leans far out of the window and LOOKS TO THE LEFT AND THEN TO THE RIGHT. Suddenly she hears the sound of horses' hoofs. SHE CLAPS HER HANDS IN JOY. She says, "AT LAST HE COMES!" But when the horse and rider come into view, it isn't her lover! It is her bitter enemy! SHE BACKS AWAY. There is THE EXPRESSION OF HORROR ON HER FACE. "NO, NO, NO!" she breathes. When he comes near she finds strength she did not know she possessed. SHE BEATS HIM WITH HER FISTS. SHE SCRATCHES HIS EYES OUT. Bleeding and beaten, he turns and runs down the trail. And then, ah, then, she sees her beloved coming. "O, DARLING!" SHE CRIES. Soon she is safe in his arms! SHE GIVES A CONTENTED SIGH. Then PUCKERS UP HER PRETTY MOUTH . . . and GIVES HIM A RESOUNDING KISS.

A Spasm in Three Speeds[4]

This is one of those stunts put on by people spontaneously called from the audience, and it is hilarious. Its success depends upon the person who leads it.

Ask the women and the girls in the audience to choose five men or boys who are the best sports they know—the kind of fellows who will do anything you ask them to do. When the five have been chosen and brought to the front of the room, announce that they are to present a famous "Shakespearean" play entitled "A Spasm in Three Speeds." Tell the audience that they will do the casting of the play by popular applause after all the characters have been named. The characters needed are:

THE KING, a stern and serious ruler

THE QUEEN, totally devoted to the King

THE BEAUTIFUL PRINCESS, who dreams of a faraway land and a handsome Prince

THE HANDSOME PRINCE, who falls madly in love with the Princess

THE PAGE, who runs errands and carries official messages for the King

Ask the five men to stand side by side, backs to the audience for the casting. Vote on the King first. Point to each of the five in turn and ask the audience to applaud the one they wish to be King. When he is chosen, tap him gently on the shoulder, turn him around facing the audience, shake his hand, and congratulate him. Ask him to step aside and be seated until the others have been chosen. Select the Queen and the other characters in the same manner the King was chosen.

When the characters have been chosen, proceed in the following manner:

[4] Adapted and used by permission of Clyde M. Maguire, Jacksonville, Florida.

FUN WITH AUDIENCE PARTICIPATION SKITS/CHAPTER 6

As our play begins, the KING is seated on the Royal Throne in the center of the stage. He sits tall and stately and holds high the Royal Scepter. *(A rolled up newspaper will do.)*

The beautiful QUEEN is sitting beside HIS MAJESTY with a hand on his shoulder, looking lovingly at him.

To the left of the KING and QUEEN, the PRINCESS is standing, leaning against the wall—dreaming of a faraway land and a handsome prince.

The PAGE and the PRINCE are outside the palace, stage right.

Although the chosen characters possess the very rarest of talents, they will still need to rehearse their lines before putting on the play. Those of you in the audience need not listen while instructions are given to the players. *(Of course, everyone will listen.)*

PAGE, as the scene opens, you march in and kneel before the KING and very seriously and dramatically say, "O KING, A STRANGER IS WITHOUT." *(Put the PAGE in place and let him repeat the line after you until he makes it melodramatic. He and the other characters will make the lines as dramatic as you motivate them to do. Be sure that all characters can be heard. Use gestures profusely.)*

KING, you answer the PAGE in kingly tones and with utter seriousness as you say, "WITHOUT WHAT?" *(Work on the KING until his line is done just right and without laughing. Without letting the audience hear you, keep reminding the characters not to laugh at themselves. This spoils the fun.)*

PAGE, your next line is, "WITHOUT THE GATE!"

KING, your next line is done in the form of a command as you say, "WELL, GIVE HIM THE GATE, AND BRING HIM IN!"

PAGE, of course you march out and bring in the waiting PRINCE.

PRINCE, as you enter the room, you see the beautiful PRINCESS, and your mission is forgotten. It is love at first sight.

PRINCESS, you too fall madly in love at the sight of the handsome PRINCE.

PRINCE, you move toward the beautiful PRINCESS as if in a

trance. Just before you reach the spot where she is standing, you turn, fall on your knees before the KING, and say with deep emotion, "O KING, I MUST MARRY THE BEAUTIFUL PRINCESS!"

QUEEN, you jump to your feet, wring your hands, and with much joy at the thought of getting rid of "the old girl," say, "O MY DARLING DAUGHTER!"

KING, you jump to your feet and shout, "CURSES, WHAT AN OUTRAGE!" Then hit the PRINCE over the head with your scepter. He falls over dead. Hit the other characters on the head and watch them die. The scene comes to a close as you dramatically sit on your throne and tragically conk yourself on the head and die.

Now, let's be sure you have your lines in mind. PAGE, you march in, bow before the KING, and say what?

(Let him do his first line and see that he does it melodramatically. Review the lines for each character. Then run the lines once without action.)

Now, audience, we are ready for the play to begin. We would remind you that it is titled, "A Spasm in Three Speeds." The first act is done in normal, everyday speed just as we usually walk and talk.

Any questions, Cast? *(Be sure all is clear before you proceed.)*

Act I

PAGE *(marching in and kneeling before the King)*: O King, a stranger is without.
KING *(in kingly tones)*: Without what?
PAGE: Without the gate!
KING: Well, give him the gate and bring him in!

(PAGE goes to waiting PRINCE and brings him to the KING. As the PRINCE enters the room, he sees the beautiful PRINCESS. It is love at first sight. He forgets the official business that brought him to the palace. He moves toward the PRINCESS as if in a trance. Just before he reaches her, he turns and falls on his knees before the KING and speaks with deep emotion.)

PRINCE: O King, I must marry your daughter!
QUEEN *(jumping to her feet):* Oh my darling daughter!
KING *(rising to his feet):* Curses! What an outrage! *(He hits the* PRINCE *on the head with his scepter. The* PRINCE *falls over dead. He dramatically hits the other characters on the head and watches them die. He then sits on his throne and tragically conks himself on the head and dies.)*

Lead the audience in applauding the players and immediately announce the second act. *(The second act is done in slow, slow motion. Walking is done in slow motion; kneeling is done in slow motion; talking, falling in love, killing, and dying are all done in slow motion.)*

Act II

(Be sure the PAGE *starts the act in slow motion. If not, stop him and start him again. The others will catch the slow motion idea if the* PAGE *does.)*

After applauding Act II, announce the third and final act, which is done in fast tempo. Everything is done just as fast as possible!

At the end of the act, the audience will of course want to once again applaud the good sports who pitched in to make it such fun!

Lion Hunt[5]

Here is a dramatic story that is fun to do with any group. The leader tells the story with exaggerated motions and sound effects,

[5]This version of the "Lion Hunt" was shared by Leon Mitchell, Church Recreation Department, Baptist Sunday School Board, Nashville, Tennessee.

142 FUN WITH AUDIENCE PARTICIPATION SKITS/CHAPTER 6

while the audience does what he does and says what he says.

Suggested actions to accompany the narrative are included in parentheses. The chorus is sung with motions and is repeated several times.

Chorus

> Go-ing on a li-on hunt. I'm not a-fraid, cause I got my gun and my bul-lets by my side.

(On the first line, pantomime the steering of an automobile. Point thumb at self on the second line.)

Narrative

So here we go. *(Alternately slap hands on knees for walking effect.)*
We open the door,
Go out on the porch, *(Repeat walking effect.)*
Shut the door, *(Slap hands together.)*
We walk to the jeep, *(Repeat walking effect.)*
And climb right in. *(Raise right leg.)*
Turn on the key, *(Reach out right hand and twist the wrist.)*
Put it in low, *(Pull back right arm.)*
Let out the clutch, *(Raise left leg.)*
And here we go. *(Slap knees again for walking effect.)*

Repeat Chorus

Narrative

Get to the spot, *(Screeching sound of car brakes.)*
Turn off the key,

Get out of the jeep,
Have a look-see, *(Place hand over eyes like an Indian looking at the horizon.)*
Let's walk to a tree, *(Repeat slapping of knees.)*
And climb that tree. *(Climb an imaginary tree by reaching upward, hand over hand to a point above the head.)*
Then we better stop
Cause we reached the top.
Look all around. *(Place hand over eyes in Indian fashion again.)*
No lions anywhere,
So we climb back down *(Reverse the hand over hand climbing motion.)*
'Till we reach the ground. *(Spread arms like umpire indicating "safe" in baseball.)*
Now we walk right along
'Till we come to a bridge.
Let's cross that bridge *(Thump the chest with closed fists in the same rhythm as walking.)*
Look over the side. *(Lean over and look down.)*
Fallllllll in. *(Make diving motions as in swimming.)*
That's O.K. *(Throw hands up as if to say, "Who cares, anyway?")*
Good day for a swim. *(Swim strokes with exaggerated motions.)*
Swim to the side.
Shake yourself off. *(Make a wiggling motion with palms of hands moving back and forth at the waist.)*
Here's the tall grass. *(Part the grass with both hands.)*
Walk right through. *(Rub hands together.)*
A great big hill *(Look at ceiling still rubbing hands together.)*
Let's climb that hill. *(Slap knees as before.)*
It's a mighty steep hill
So we better slow down. *(Use slow, deliberate slaps on knees.)*

Repeat Chorus
(sing slower and slower while slapping knees)

Narrative

There's a cave over there.
Let's look inside.
(Cups hands) It's mighty dark in here.
I don't see a thing!

Repeat Chorus

(cupped hands)

Narrative

What's that? *(Look over shoulder.)*
Two big eyes, *(Look frightened.)*
Furry head, *(Hands cupped above head.)*
Lots of teeth, *(Grit the teeth.)*
Shaggy mane, *(Make stroking motions.)*
Broad back, *(Extend arms out to each side.)*
Long tail, *(Make an upward sweep of the right arm behind the back.)*
IT'S A LION!!!!!! *(Place fingers between the teeth.)*
(much faster) Run out of that cave. *(Slap knees as before and do everything in reverse order.)*
Run down the hill.
Don't look back. *(Shake head vigorously.)*
He's following us still.
Run through the tall grass,
And across that bridge.
Fallllllllll in.
Start to swim.
Climb out the other side.
Shake yourself off.
Run to the tree.
Climb that tree.
Look all around. *(Pause, and breathe as if exhausted.)*
Not a lion anywhere.
(slower) So I climb back down,

And I walk to the jeep.
Climb in,
Turn on the key,
Put it in low,
Let out the clutch,
And home we go.

Repeat Chorus
(using past tense)

Narrative

Stop!!!! *(Screeching sound of car brakes as before.)*
What's that?
Two big eyes,
Furry head,
Lots of teeth,
Shaggy mane,
Broad back,
Long tail,
It's a LION!!!!!
It's in the jeep!!!!!
Jump out of the jeep!
Run to the house!
Open the door!
Jump inside!
Close the door!
Run upstairs,
Jump under the bed! *(Put hands together as if diving into a swimming pool. Jump flat-footed, leaving the floor.)*
Hide my head! *(Bend over forward and put both hands behind the head.)*

Repeat Chorus
(softly and SLOWLY, *hands on head)*

Narrative

What's that?
Two big eyes,
Furry head,
Lots of teeth,
Shaggy mane,
Broad back,
Long tail,
IT'S A LION!!!!!
Oh, well!
That's O.K.
He's here to stay.
Let's not fret.
He's my big fat pet! *(Extend arms and hands in exaggerated manner to indicate a fat person.)*

Repeat Chorus
(use past tense)

Narrative

Gonna go again,
But not today,
Cause I done been! *(Wipe the brow in relief.)*

CHAPTER SEVEN

CHORAL SPEAKING

One of the most delightful fun times the author ever experienced was a fifty-minute program of choral speaking presented in summer camp by junior high boys and girls. They spent many happy hours rehearsing over a period of weeks, and their presentation added a real spark of excitement to the camp program.

If properly done, the fun aspects of choral speaking appeal to all ages. The very same nonsensical piece to which a child responds also appeals to the adult who needs a momentary release from the serious and weighty matters of life.

The selections included in this chapter have been successfully done by adults, college students, senior high and junior high youth, and older children.

Interpretation suggestions are shared for the first three poems. The other pieces which are included will need to be worked out by the director in a similar manner if the lines are to communicate the intended message.

Suggestions for the Director

Here are some simple suggestions for the inexperienced director:

1. Choose material that you like and can really have fun doing. Your excitement and enthusiasm will be caught by those with whom you work.

2. It is a good idea to have in mind a specific presentation date, even before enlisting your people. This target can be a constant source of motivation.

3. Carefully study your material before calling people together to work on it. The only basis for vocal expression must be in a thorough understanding of the meaning of the piece.

4. Choral speaking can be done with two or more people. The larger the number, the bigger the group sound can be. A good sound can be achieved with eight to fifteen people.

5. At the first rehearsal, work in jingles until your group is able to

BEGIN together,
SPEAK at the same rate of speed, and
FINISH at the same split second.

The first line of "Peter Piper" is a good one to begin with. When togetherness has been established, move to a humorous selection of poetry or prose and begin work on it. Remember, make it fun!

6. Lead the group to study the piece. Until they understand the selection, they cannot impart it to an audience. The following procedure will help in the study of a passage:

(1) One person reads aloud to the group or all read silently.
(2) Discuss the selection.
   a. Who is the speaker?
   b. What is the setting?
   c. Under what conditions was the piece written?
   d. What is the theme? What is the author trying to say? Explain the central idea of the piece.
   e. Define new words.
   f. Clear up vague meanings.
   g. Lead the group to agree on a unity of thought. When lines can be interpreted to mean different things, the ideas of the majority must prevail.

7. Avoid the pitfall of a sing-song, dull, monotonous reading. Work for variety.

8. Work for a memorized performance in which the group is so prepared that they need no assistance from the director. Only then can excitement and total animation be achieved.

Evolution

Author Unknown

ALL *(facing the audience and speaking as a storyteller to catch the attention of the audience and give the setting of the drama):*

> Some monkeys sat in a coconut tree,
> discussing things as they're said to be.
> Said one to the others,

SOLO *(imaginatively becoming a monkey for the moment and looking at the other monkeys as he voices his concern and shares the rumor he has heard):*
> Now listen, you,
> There's a certain rumor that can't be true—
> That man descended from our Noble Race.

BOYS *(shocked):* The very idea!
GIRLS *(outraged):* It's a dire disgrace!
(The following lines build one on the other in rapid succession, each one mounting in intensity and excitement. The monkeys must be totally unaware of the audience and must react to one another and to each statement that is made.)
BOYS: No monkey ever deserted his wife.
GIRLS: Starved her baby
ALL: And ruined her life.
SOLO: And you've never known a mother monk to leave her baby with others to bunk
SOLO: Or pass them on from one to another
ALL: 'Till they hardly know who is their mother.
SOLO: And another thing you will never see,
a monk build a fence around a coconut tree.
ALL: And let the coconuts go to waste,
forbidding all other monks a taste.

SOLO:	Why, if I put up a fence around this tree,
	Starvation would force you to steal from me.
GIRLS:	Here's another thing a monk won't do,
BOYS:	Go out at night and get on a stew
SOLO:	Or use a gun or club or knife
	To take some other monkey's life.
ALL	*(facing audience):* Yes! Man descended, the ORNERY cuss, But brother, he didn't descend from us!

(Work for an informal arrangement with some standing, others seated upon the backs of chairs, etc. Some are totally turned toward the audience and others partially facing the audience. Be sure each person can be seen and understood by the audience.)

I Know an Old Woman[1]

(adapted from the poem by Mrs. Klaus Grabe)

SOLO 1   *(speaking to the others in the choral speaking group who immediately focus on him at his first word, he gives the impression that what he is saying is perhaps the most unusual thing that's ever happened to anybody):*

I know an old woman who swallowed a fly!

ALL   *(with unbelief):* A fly?
I don't know WHY she swallowed a fly
(sadly) I guess she'll die.

SOLO 2   *(speaking to the others in the group and topping the story just told):*

---

[1]From *Charm*, December, 1949, pp. 94-95. Used by permission.

FUN WITH CHORAL SPEAKING/CHAPTER 7

          I know an old woman who swallowed a *spider*
          that *wiggled,* and *jiggled,* and *tickled* inside her!
ALL   *(to audience):* She swallowed the spider to catch the fly.
          (much concerned) I don't know WHY she swallowed
          the fly.
          I guess she'll die.
SOLO 3 *(colors his story as if to say, "Well, what the others*
          have told is kid stuff. Just listen to this!"):
          I know an old woman who swallowed a *bird!*
ALL   *(totally surprised):* A *bird?*
          (still focusing on Soloist 3):
          How absurd to swallow a bird!
          (facing audience) She swallowed the bird
          to catch the spider that tickled inside her.
          She swallowed the spider to catch the fly.
          (with mounting concern each time the following phrase
          appears)
          I don't know WHY she swallowed the fly.
          I guess she'll die.
          (Each succeeding soloist outdoes the previous one in
          making his story a bigger one. The volume, color, and
          excitement must increase each time.)
SOLO 4: *I* know an old woman who swallowed a *cat!*
ALL: A *cat?*
          Imagine that! Swallowed a cat!
          (facing audience)
          She swallowed the cat to catch the bird.
          She swallowed the bird to catch the spider
          that tickled inside her.
          She swallowed the spider to catch the fly.
          I don't know WHY she swallowed the fly.
          I guess she'll die.
SOLO 5: *I* know an old woman who swallowed a *dog!*
ALL   *(in utter disbelief):* A dog?
          What a hog to swallow a dog!

>   *(facing audience)*
>   She swallowed the dog to catch the cat.
>   She swallowed the cat to catch the bird.
>   She swallowed the bird to catch the spider
>   that tickled inside her.
>   She swallowed the spider to catch the fly.
>   I don't know WHY she swallowed the fly.
>   I guess she'll die.
> Solo 6:   *I* know an old woman who swallowed a *cow!*
> All: A cow?
>   I don't know how she swallowed a cow!
>   *(facing audience)*
>   She swallowed the cow to catch the dog.
>   She swallowed the dog to catch the cat.
>   She swallowed the cat to catch the bird.
>   She swallowed the bird to catch the spider
>   that tickled inside her.
>   She swallowed the spider to catch the fly.
>   I don't know WHY she swallowed the fly.
>   I guess she'll die.
> Solo 7   *(topping all stories that have been told):*
>   Why, *I* know an old woman who swallowed a *horse!*
> All   *(total response of shock and disbelief):*
>   A *horse?*
> Solo 7   *(still focusing on the others in the group):*
>   Well ... she's *dead,* of course!

The Eskimo[2]

> All   *(facing audience and speaking with the "once upon a time" storytelling quality):*

---

[2]From the song "The Eskimo," copyrighted 1926 by Theo Presser Co. Used by permission.

	Upon Arctic Avenue within his hut of snow
	There lived a LONELY little Eskimo.
	Now just across the avenue and very close to this
	Within a half a mile or so there lived an Eski-Miss.
GIRLS	*(face the boys on the word "looked" and show the audience how the little Eski-Miss looked at the cute little Eskimo.*
	The whole body must become involved):
	She LOOKED at him—
BOYS	*(turning to girls on the word "looked" and showing much interest!):*
	He LOOKED at her,
ALL	*(turning to audience):*
	And underneath their furs they felt their hearts go pitty-pitty-pat.
BOYS:	Both HIS,
GIRLS:	And HERS!
ALL	*(still looking at the audience and sharing more of the story):*
	The Eskimo he loved her so, he took his little sled
	And he tucked her in, in front of him, and this is what he said:
BOYS	*(falling on their knees, facing the girls and looking up at them. They use the hands and entire body to plead their cause):*
	"Eski-Honey, Eski-Honey, Eski-Honey sweet.
	Please to leave your Eski-Pop, and move across the street."
GIRLS	*(quickly and happily accepting the proposal):*
	"We'll be very happy in our little hut of snow
	And we'll never give an ESKI-HOOT for winds that blow."
BOYS	*(still playing to the girls and using deep manly tones):*
	"And I'll go out each Eski-morn and catch an Eski-whale."

GIRLS:	"And I shall take the rest of him and you shall have the tail."
ALL:	"And when the day is over and our work is done We'll RUB our Eski-noses 'neath the Midnight Sun!" *(facing audience and once again telling more of the story)* The Eskimo he loved her so he couldn't even think. He couldn't eat his dinner and he couldn't sleep a wink, So he called upon the Eski-Miss to take her for a stroll And as the day was rather nice, they walked around the Pole!
BOYS	*(still facing audience):* Now the Eskimo he didn't know the very nicest way To tell the little Eski-Miss the things he had to say.
GIRLS	*(act out this line by winking at the boys):* But when she winked an Eski-wink to show she understood This is what he whispered in that Eski-Lady's hood:
BOYS	*(falling down again and using the exact same hand movements):* "Eski-Honey, Eski-Honey, Eski-Honey sweet. Please to leave your Eski-Pop, and move across the street. You shall have a fancy coat of very finest seal And you can tell your lady friends you're sure it's real. And I will build and keep the fires and whistle Eski-tunes."
GIRLS	*(quickly):* "While I am sewing buttons on your Sunday Eski-loons."
ALL	*(facing audience):* "And when the day is over and our work is done, *(girls and boys facing each other)* We'll RUB our Eski-noses *(facing audience)* 'neath the Midnight Sun."

(The success of this piece depends upon the degree to which those in the choral speaking group throw themselves into this delightful little tale. They must get a mental picture of all that happens and then, for the moment, imaginatively become the Eskimo *and* Eski-miss.*)*

"Local Frog Stages Comeback"

Author Unknown

Solo 1:	Two gay young frogs from inland bogs
	Had spent the night in drinking—
Girls:	As morning broke and they awoke—
	While still their eyes were blinking,
Boys:	The farmer's pail came to the swale
	And caught them quick as winking.
All:	'Ere they could gather scattered senses,
	Or breathe a prayer for past offenses,
Solo 2:	The farmer, quick, fast-working man
All:	Had dumped them in the milkman's can,
Boys:	The can filled up,
Girls:	The lid went down
All:	And soon they started off to town.
Solo 2:	They see that life will quickly stop
All:	Unless they swim upon the top;
Girls:	They swim for life, they kick and swim
Boys:	'Till their weary eyes grow dim.
Solo 3:	"Say, old top,"
All:	Says one poor sport,
Solo 3:	"I can no longer hold the fort.
	I've no more kicks in life, why try it?
	I wasn't reared on a milk diet."

Solo 4:	"Tut, tut, my lad,"
All:	The other cries,
Solo 4:	"A frog's not dead until he dies!
	Keep on kicking, that's my plan
	We may yet see outside this can."
Solo 3:	"No use, no use,"
All:	Faint-Heart replied,
	Turned up his toes and gently died.
Solo 1:	The other frog undaunted still
Boys:	Kept on kicking with a right good will—
Solo 2:	Until with joy too great to utter
Girls:	He found he'd churned a pound of butter.
Solo 1:	And climbing on that hunk of grease,
Boys:	He floated to town with the greatest of ease.
All:	Moral: When times are hard and you would frown
Girls:	Don't get discouraged and go down—
Boys:	Just struggle on, no murmur utter,
All:	One more kick may bring the butter.

A Youngster Named Danny
(Anonymous)

Solo 1:	There once was a youngster named Danny,
All:	Who tackled a big, ripe bananny;
Girls:	The thing was so slick
Boys:	And it slipped down so quick
All:	He got scared and he yelled for his mammy.
Solo 2:	And Mammy, she hollered for Annie,
Solo 3:	And Annie roared loudly for Fannie:
Girls:	And Fannie and Annie
Boys:	Helped Mammy stand Danny
All:	On his head, and shake out the bananny!

A Tree Toad Loved a She-Toad

Author Unknown

Solo 1:	A tree toad loved a she-toad
	That lived up in a tree
Girls:	She was a three-toed tree toad
Boys:	But a two-toed toad was he.
Solo 2:	The two-toed tree toad tried to win
	The three-toed toad's friendly nod.
Boys:	For the two-toed tree toad loved the ground
Girls:	The three-toed tree toad trod.
Solo 3:	Vainly the two-toed tree toad tried,
Boys:	But he couldn't please her whim.
Girls:	In her tree toad bower;
Boys:	With her V-toed power,
All:	The she-toad vetoed him.

Definition of a Boy

Anonymous

(It will be fun to have this piece done by girls only.)

Solo:	A boy is—
Group 1:	A piece of skin stretched over an appetite.
Group 2:	A noise covered with smudges.
All:	He is called a tornado
Solo 2:	Because he comes at the most unexpected times,
Solo 3:	Hits the most unexpected places,
All:	And leaves everything a wreck behind him.

Solo 1: He is part human,
Solo 2: Part angel,
Solo 3: And part barbarian.
Group 1: He is a growing animal of superlative promise,
All: To be fed, watered, and kept warm.
Solo 1: A joy forever,
Solo 2: A periodic nuisance,
Group 1: The problem of our times,
Group 2: The hope of the nation.
All: Every new boy born is evidence that God is not yet discouraged with man.

I Had a Hippopotamus[3]

Patrick Barrington

All: I had a hippopotamus; I kept him in a shed
And fed him up on vitamins and vegetable bread;
Solo 1: I made him my companion on many cheery walks
Solo 2: And had his portrait done by a celebrity in chalks.
Solo 3: His charming eccentricities were known on every side,
The creature's popularity was wonderfully wide;
Solo 4: He frolicked with the Rector in a dozen friendly tussles,
Who could not but remark upon his hippopotamuscles.
Solo 5: If he should be afflicted by depression or the dumps,
By hippopotameasles or the hippopotamumps,
All: I never knew a particle of peace till it was plain
He was hippopotamasticating properly again.

[3]From *Punch* (London), July 21, 1933. Used by permission.

FUN WITH CHORAL SPEAKING/CHAPTER 7

ALL: I had a hippopotamus; I loved him as a friend;
But beautiful relationships are bound to have an end.
SOLO 6: Time takes, alas! our joys from us
and robs us of our blisses;
My hippopotamus turned out a hippopotamissis.
SOLO 7: My housekeeper regarded him with jaundice in her eye;
She did not want a colony of hippopotami;
SOLO 8: She borrowed a machine-gun from her soldier-nephew, Percy,
And showed my hippopotamus no hippopotamercy.
ALL: My house now lacks the glamour that the charming creature gave,
The garage where I kept him is as silent as the grave;
SOLO 9: No longer he displays among the motor-tyres and spanners
His hippopotamastery of hippopotamanners.
SOLO 10: No longer now he gambols in the orchard in the Spring
No longer do I lead him through the village on a string;
ALL: No longer in the mornings does the neighborhood rejoice
To his hippopotamusically-modulated voice.
ALL: I had a hippopotamus; but nothing upon earth
Is constant in its happiness or lasting in its mirth.
No joy that life can give me can be strong enough to smother
My sorrow for the might-have-been-a-hippopotamother.

A Fly and a Flea[4]

Solo 1:	A fly and a flea in a flue
Boys:	Were imprisoned, so what could they do?
All:	Said the fly,
Solo 2:	"Let us flee."
All:	Said the flea
Solo 3:	"Let us fly."
All:	So they flew through a flaw in the flue.

Breaking the Ice

(Author Unknown)

Solo 1:	Slippery ice,
Solo 2:	Very thin,
Boys:	Pretty girl tumbled in.
Girls:	Saw a boy on the bank,
Solo 3:	Gave a shriek,
Boys:	And then she sank.
Solo 2:	Boy on bank heard her shout,
Girls:	Jumped right in and pulled her out.
Boys:	Now they're married,
Girls:	Very nice!
All:	But *she* had to break the ice.

---

[4]From *Lots of Limericks*, ed. Louis Untermeyer (New York: Doubleday & Co., 1961). Used by permission.

The Two Frogs

Author Unknown

ALL:	Two frogs fell into a milk pail deep,
DUET:	Gr-r-r-rump, gr-r-r-rump, gr-r-r-rump!
GIRLS:	And one poor frog did nothing but weep.
BOYS:	He sank to the bottom as heavy as lead,
ALL:	And there in the morning they found him dead.
SOLO 1:	Gump, gump, gump!
BOYS:	The other frog shouted,
SOLO 2:	"I'll have a good try. The pail may be deep, but I don't want to die."
SOLO 3:	Gr-r-r-rump, gr-r-r-rump, gr-r-r-rump!
GIRLS:	He churned up the milk with his legs fore and hind—
ALL:	There's nothing like having a masterful mind,
BOYS:	For when the next morning this Froggy was found,
GIRLS:	On a pat of fresh butter he floated around.
ALL:	Gr-r-r-r-room, gr-r-r-r-room, gr-r-r-r-room!

On Being a Senior Adult

(Author Unknown)

SOLO 1:	There's nothing on earth the matter with me,
ALL:	I'm just as healthy as I can be.
SOLO 2:	I have arthritis in both my knees
GIRLS:	And when I talk,
BOYS:	I talk with a wheeze.
SOLO 3:	My pulse is weak,
SOLO 4:	And my blood is thin.

ALL:	But I'm awfully well for the shape I'm in.
SOLO 1:	My remaining teeth will soon fall out.
SOLO 2:	And my diet—
GIRLS:	I hate to talk about.
SOLO:	I'm overweight and I can't get thin.
BOYS:	My appetite's such that I know it'll win.
ALL:	But I'm awfully well for the shape I'm in.
SOLO 3:	Arch supports I have for my feet—
ALL:	Or I wouldn't be able to go on the street.
SOLO 4:	Sleep is denied me night after night,
BOYS:	And every morning—
GIRLS:	I am a sight!
SOLO 5:	My memory is failing,
SOLO 6:	My head's in a spin,
SOLO 7:	I'm practically living on aspirin.
ALL:	But I'm awfully well for the shape I'm in.
SOLO 1:	"Old age is golden,"
GIRLS:	I've heard it said,
SOLO 2:	But sometimes I wonder as I go to bed.
GIRLS:	My ears in the drawer,
BOYS:	My teeth in a cup,
SOLO 3:	My eyes on the table until I get up.
SOLO 4:	As sleep finally comes, I say to myself,
ALL:	"Is there anything else I should put on the shelf?"
SOLO 5:	But I'm happy to say as I close the door,
ALL:	My friends are the same as in days of yore.
SOLO 6:	I get up each morning,
SOLO 7:	Dust off my wits,
ALL:	Pick up the paper and read the obits.
SOLO 1:	If my name isn't there,
SOLO 2:	I know I'm not dead.
ALL:	So, I eat a good breakfast, then go back to bed!

CHAPTER EIGHT

IMPROMPTU SKITS

There is no end to what can be done by dividing people into small groups and giving each group an idea on which to build a fun drama. No advance preparation is made except by the director.

The real fun comes in the small groups as they create their skits. Barriers are broken down, and individuals really get to know one another in this informal setting. Each person has an opportunity to contribute, and even the shy ones can quickly become a part of the group.

Give the participants at least twenty minutes to plan, cast their dramas, and rehearse. Then let them perform. Be sure to allow at least forty-five minutes for preparation and the presentations.

Here are fourteen suggested ways to involve groups in creating their own fun skits:

1. SITUATION DRAMA

Give each group this situation or one you will create and ask them to dramatize it:

Joe, somebody they all know and love, was walking down the street when he saw a woman standing at the bus stop. He thought it was someone he knew, so he slipped up behind her and covered her eyes with his hands to make her guess who it was. The woman turned around, saw Joe, and screamed for help. Just at that moment, a policeman came around the corner.

Each group is to act out the story, adding their own imaginative thinking as to what happened to their friend Joe.

2. BEGIN WITH COMMERCIAL SIGNS

Announce that each group will be given three commercial signs around which their skit is to be created. After dividing into groups, hold up the signs you have available and let them choose the ones that spark their imagination. Cardboard signs can be purchased from the Variety Store or they can be easily made. They may include the following:

> NO SOLICITING
> NO TRESPASSING
> FOR RENT
> COME IN, WE'RE OPEN
> SORRY, WE'RE CLOSED
> EXIT
> ROOMS
> HELP WANTED
> BEWARE OF DOG
> NO PARKING
> KEEP OUT
> FIRE ESCAPE
> FOR SALE
> KEEP OFF THE GRASS
> DAY SLEEPER
> OUT OF ORDER

3. WORD STARTERS

Some of the best skits are created from a single word. Assign each group a set of words similar to the following:

FUN WITH IMPROMPTU SKITS/CHAPTER 8

A shot, a scream
mortgage, hero
kidnapped, gypsies
jewels, stolen
dark cave, lost
the body, found
midnight, telephone
storm, candle
attic, chains
blood, locked door
smoke, stairway
match, hidden treasure
sheriff, nylon stocking
imposter, prince

4. ACT OUT OLD SAYINGS

Give each group three old sayings which they must weave into their skit. Use the ones from the following list that will be most familiar to the particular age group:

(1) bitter as gall
(2) proud as a peacock
(3) ugly as sin
(4) poor as a church mouse
(5) busy as a bee
(6) flat as a pancake
(7) strong as an ox
(8) white as snow
(9) sharp as a razor
(10) thin as a rail
(11) stiff as a poker
(12) quiet as a mouse
(13) fat as a pig
(14) green as grass

(15) hard as a rock
(16) heavy as lead
(17) red as a beet
(18) neat as a pin
(19) dry as a bone
(20) deep as the ocean
(21) crazy as a loon
(22) full as a tick
(23) dead as a doornail
(24) light as a feather
(25) hot as fire
(26) blind as a bat
(27) fine as a fiddle
(28) sweet as honey
(29) big as an elephant
(30) sly as a fox
(31) pretty as a picture
(32) quick as lightning
(33) brave as a lion
(34) tight as a drum
(35) black as coal

5. RADIO AND TV COMMERCIALS

Ask each group to choose a product of a ridiculous nature and create a singing commercial and brief sales speech (not more than three minutes), possibly including a word from a "satisfied customer."

In advance, prepare a list of suggested products such as Granny's Greasy Goulash, Lucy's Lumbago Liniment, and Scrapo Shaving Cream. As groups show off their creative genius, make a tape recording. Be sure to allow sufficient time in the schedule for the playback, because this is where the real fun begins.

6. OLD-FASHIONED RECITATIONS

Remind the participants of the old-fashioned, melodramatic recitations that in earlier days played such an important part in schools and in community life. Tell them that they're going to have the privilege of seeing what the "old days" were like by taking part in a recitation contest.

Ask each group to choose a boy and a girl to represent them. Each contestant is to recite "Mary Had a Little Lamb" or "Twinkle, Twinkle, Little Star" as one of the following characters would do it:

>A barker at a circus
>A gossip
>A five-year-old
>A lisping girl or boy
>Grandma or grandpa with no teeth
>A would-be actress
>A stutterer
>A train announcer
>A politician
>A society girl
>A bashful boy
>A person with a nasal twang

After each contestant has decided which character he will be, his group will listen to him, offer suggestions on how to make it funnier, and let him try it again. Of course, gestures should be used profusely!

Add to the fun by awarding plaques which can be made out of paper plates lettered with a Magic Marker.

7. BEGIN WITH A SET OF CHARACTERS

Assign each group a set of characters from which they are to weave a plot, rehearse, secure props, and produce a three- to five-minute play. Suggested characters:

> a cowboy, a waitress, and a gangster
> policeman, a man selling pencils, a dog
> a taxicab driver, a nurse, an old woman
> a blind man, a doctor, and a victim of amnesia
> a movie star, a bum, and a gypsy
> a deaf old woman, a deaf old man, a salesman
> newspaper boy, bandit, policeman

8. UNRELATED SENTENCES

Furnish each group with two or three unrelated sentences which must be woven into the lines of a fun skit:

> Keep quiet and they'll never know we're here!
> But who'll dig the hole?
> He always did like fried okra.
> Poor Algernon, he always was fond of snakes!

9. PAPER SACK PUPPETS

Supply each group with paper sacks, Crayolas, Magic Markers, or tempera paint. They are to make puppet heads out of the sacks and create a puppet show. When the features have been painted on, blow up the sacks and tie them with string, leaving enough of the sack below the string for a handle with which to work the puppet.

10. PAPER BAG DRAMA

Supply each group with a large paper bag containing several costume pieces. Their skit is to be woven around the costumes in the bag. Each piece must be utilized in the skit.

11. UNRELATED OBJECTS

Give to each group three unrelated objects around which a drama must be built. They may be a toy pistol, a pair of dark glasses, and a woman's purse. A closet or attic will reveal many possible objects to use.

12. ACT OUT FAIRY STORIES

Give each group the story of "Red Riding Hood," "Goldilocks and the Three Bears," or some other well-known fairy tale and ask them to do a modern version in the form of a skit.

13. ACT OUT NURSERY RHYMES

Assign each group a nursery rhyme such as "Little Miss Muffet" and ask them to act out what *really* happened. Was it *really* a spider that sat down beside her and was she *really* scared away?

14. ACT OUT PROVERBS

Give each group a list of proverbs and let them choose one from which they will create their skit. The following proverbs offer many possibilities for fun dramas:

List of Proverbs

1. Birds of a feather flock together.
2. Absence makes the heart grow fonder.
3. Too many cooks spoil the broth.
4. Spare the rod and spoil the child.
5. Like father, like son.
6. Children should be seen, not heard.
7. Haste makes waste.

8. A new broom sweeps clean.
9. It is better to be sure than sorry.
10. Everybody's business is nobody's business.
11. A penny saved is a penny earned.
12. Never cry over spilt milk.
13. A watched pot never boils.
14. Leave well enough alone.
15. Strike while the iron is hot.
16. A wise man changes his mind, but a fool never.
17. A bird in hand is worth two in the bush.
18. Practice makes perfect.
19. Honesty is the best policy.
20. You can lead a horse to water, but you cannot make him drink.
21. No fool like an old fool.
22. A friend in need is a friend indeed.
23. It is too late to lock the stable door when the steed is stolen.
24. Make hay while the sun shines.
25. Procrastination is the thief of time.
26. Barking dogs never bite.
27. You can't teach an old dog new tricks.
28. Paddle your own canoe.
29. 'Tis better to have loved and lost than never to have loved at all.—Tennyson
30. It is best to let sleeping dogs lie.
31. Misery loves company.
32. Necessity is the mother of invention.
33. Every dog has his day.
34. He labors in vain who tries to please everybody.
35. Two heads are better than one.
36. Cold hand, a warm heart.
37. Fools' names as well as faces
    Are often seen in public places
38. Wherever there is smoke there is fire.

39. Easy come, easy go.
40. Familiarity breeds contempt.
41. Experience is the best teacher.
42. We learn to do by doing.
43. A stitch in time saves nine.
44. You can't have your cake and eat it too.
45. While there is life there is hope.
46. The road to hell is paved with good intentions.
47. Practice what you preach.
48. Never put off until tomorrow what you can do today.
49. A rolling stone gathers no moss.
50. Fools rush in where angels fear to tread.
51. The proof of the pudding is in the eating.
52. Easier said than done.
53. Jack of all trades and master of none.
54. If at first you don't succeed, try, try again.
55. Never count your chickens before they are hatched.
56. A word to the wise is sufficient.
57. Still water runs deep.
58. Every cloud has a silver lining.
59. Actions speak louder than words.
60. The early bird catches the worm.
61. Beggars must not be choosers.
62. One rotten apple spoils the whole barrel.
63. The burnt child dreads the fire.
64. When the cat's away the mice will play.
65. As the twig is bent the tree's inclined.
66. Early to bed and early to rise
Makes a man healthy, wealthy, and wise.—Franklin
67. Turn about is fair play.
68. Beauty is but skin deep.
69. Who the daughter would win
With mamma must begin.
70. Never ride a free horse to death.
71. He who laughs last laughs best.

72. Variety's the very spice of life
    That gives it all its flavor.—Cowper
73. Nothing ventured; nothing gained.
74. If wishes were horses, beggars would ride.

INDEX

Abigail Stands Fast (melodrama), 78
Acknowledgments, 7
Act out fairy stories, 169
Act out nursery rhymes, 169
Act out old sayings, 165
Act out proverbs, 169
Audience participation Skits, 131

Balloon music (Musical Balloon), 26
Banana Feed, 35
Begin with a set of characters, 167
Begin with commercials, 164
Biscuit-making contest (A kitchen drama), 17
Blind art, 36
Blind banana feed, 35
Blown with the Breeze (melodrama), 86
Bottle orchestra, 33
Boxer (An Interview with Punchy McPugg), 59
Breaking the Ice (choral speaking), 160

Can'tsee Poorsight, 38
Carmen (mock opera), 104
Choir skits, 96
Choosing the material to be used, 11
Choral speaking, 147
Choral speaking techniques, 147
Christmas, 65
Clap Rhythm, 26
Comb orchestra, 25
Commercial signs (Begin with commercial signs), 164
Contents, 9
Cool conversation (ice stunt), 17
"Country Gardens" Rhythm, 33
Creating your own skits, 163

Definition of a boy (choral speaking), 157
Doctor Quack's Medicine Show (musical skit), 120
Doll Shop, 20

Drama in three speeds, 138
Dress that mannequin, 36

Easter hat show, 34
Echo, 34
Elephant pantomime (Washing an elephant) 15
Eskimo (choral speaking), 152
Evolution (choral speaking), 149

Fake fortune-telling, 37
Fashion preview, 18
Fatal Quest, 42
Feather Weight Champ, (melodrama), 90
Fly and a Flea (choral speaking), 160
Fortune telling, 37
Four choice, 31
Frog stages comeback (choral speaking), 155
Frogs (The Two Frogs, choral speaking), 161
From Nine to Five, 61
Fun with audience participation skits, 131
Fun with choral speaking, 147
Fun with Hamlet and his friends (monologue), 45
Fun with impromptu skits, 163
Fun with melodrama, 78
Fun with musical skits, 96
Fun with tongue twisters, 24

Get out there and fight, 23
Gransel and Hettal, 73

Hail, King Bo Bo, 21
Halloween, 69
Hamlet and His Friends (monologue), 45
Hat modeling, 34
Hat show, 34
Henry (monologue), 48
Hideous creature (the only one in captivity), 15

Hippopotamus (choral speaking), 158
Hunter, gun, rabbit, 20

Ice stunt, 17
Identify that nose, 25
I had a hippopotamus (choral speaking), 158
I know an old woman (choral speaking), 150
Impromptu Skits, 163
Interview with Punchy McPugg, 59
It shouldn't happen to a dog (musical skit), 108
King Bo Bo, 21
King with the terrible temper, 135
Kissing the King's ring, 21
Kitchen Drama (biscuit-making contest), 17

Lion Hunt, 141
Local Frog Stages Comeback (choral speaking), 155
Lover's Errand, 52

Magic writing, 31
Magician act, 32
Magician in our midst, 27
Making a movie (The Stand-in), 40
Mannequin dressing contest, 36
Medicine show, 120
"Mellerdrammer", 84
Melodrama, 78
Mind reading, 29
Miss America, 16
Mock Opera, 96
Monologues, 45
Moon is round, 19
Musical balloon, 26
Musical skits, 96
Mysterious echo, 34

Necktie stunt, 27
Night before Christmas, 65
Nobility, 131
Nose identification, 25

Novelty stunts, 14
Nursery rhymes, 169

Old-fashioned recitations, 167
Old sayings, 165
Old Woman (choral speaking), 150
On being a Senior Adult (choral speaking), 161
Only one in captivity, 15
Othello (mock opera), 96

Papa shot a bear, 35
Paper bag drama, 168
Paper sack art, 36
Paper sack puppets, 168
Peanut Butter (monologue), 49
Pillow case drama, 23
Preface, 7
Prepared skits, 38
Preparing the material to be used, 12
Presentation Pointers, 13
Proverbs, a list of 75, 169
Punchy McPugg, 59
Puppets, 168
Pure White (monologue), 50

Radio and TV Commercials, 166
Recitations (Old-fashioned recitations), 167
Rhyme's the Crime (melodrama), 92
Romance of Minnie Martin (musical skit), 108
Russian Quartet, 54

Senior Adult (On Being a Senior Adult), 161
Shadow plays, 18
Shaving Stunt, 14
Situation drama, 163
Sofapillio, 55
Spasm in Three Speeds, 138
Sports Skit (Interview with Punchy McPugg), 59
Stand-in, 40

Starring You (audience participation skit), 137
Story of Gransel and Hettal, 73

Temple reading, 30
Tickled to Death (melodrama), 90
Tied-feminine style, 27
Tongue-twisters, 24
Touch reading, 30
Tree Toad Loved a She-Toad (choral speaking), 157
Trip to Mexico, 133
Two Frogs (choral speaking), 161

Unrelated objects, 169
Unrelated sentences, 168

Washing an elephant, 15
Western Stunt (The Stand-in), 40
Witches and the Crows, 69
Word starters, 164
World-famous magician, 32

Youngster named Danny (choral speaking), 156